STRANGE PICTURES

UKETSU

Translated from the Japanese by Jim Rion

T0281984

HARPERVIA

An Imprint of HarperCollins*Publishers*

HENNA E. Copyright © 2022 by Uketsu. English translation copyright © 2025 by Jim
Rion. English translation rights arranged with Futabasha Publishers Ltd. through
Japan UNI Agency, Inc., Tokyo, and Pushkin Press Limited. All rights reserved.
Printed in the United States of America. No part of this book may be used or
reproduced in any manner whatsoever without written permission except in the
case of brief quotations embodied in critical articles and reviews. For information,
address HarperCollins Publishers, 195 Broadway, New York, NY 10007.

HarperCollins books may be purchased for educational, business,
or sales promotional use. For information, please email the Special
Markets Department at SPsales@harpercollins.com.

Originally published as HENNA E in Japan in 2022
by Futabasha Publishers Ltd., Tokyo.

FIRST HARPERVIA EDITION PUBLISHED IN 2025

Design adapted from the UK edition designed and typeset by Tetragon, London.

Library of Congress Cataloging-in-Publication Data has been applied for.

ISBN 978-0-06-343308-3
ISBN 978-0-06-343309-0 (Library Edition)

24 25 26 27 28 LBC 5 4 3 2 1

'All right, everyone, now I'm going to show you a picture.'

The professor, Dr Tomiko Hagio, fixed a sheet of paper onto the classroom's blackboard.

She pointed at the drawing on it as she spoke.

'As you well know, I now dedicate my time to teaching, but before I started lecturing young people like yourselves, I cut my teeth as a practising psychologist. I offered therapy to quite a number of patients over the course of my career. This picture is a copy of a drawing done by a patient I treated early on. A young girl. Let's refer to her as "Little A" for now. When Little A was eleven years old, she was arrested for the murder of her mother.'

Her words sent a ripple of shock through the students.

'I decided to administer a drawing test when undertaking her analysis. A drawing test requires that we have the patient follow a drawing prompt and use the results to analyse the patient's mental state. Like they say, "Painting is a mirror of the soul," and a drawing can often offer valuable insight into the mind of its artist. In particular, drawings of houses, trees and people tend to be remarkably revealing. Now, does anyone find anything about this picture strange?'

Dr Hagio surveyed the classroom.

The students only stared intently at the picture on the blackboard, wearing puzzled expressions.

'Does nothing stand out? At first glance, yes, it probably looks rather ordinary. But here and there pop up some very unusual points indeed. First, look closely at the girl in the centre of the drawing. Her mouth, in particular.'

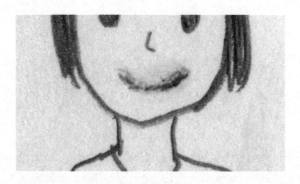

Dr Hagio pointed at it. 'It's somewhat messy and smudged. Little A had difficulty getting the mouth right, having to redraw it many times. She managed to get the other features down in a single go, so why did she keep making mistakes at the mouth? This offers us a clue to understanding her state of mind.

'Little A was abused by her mother,' Dr Hagio elaborated. 'It seems that whenever she was home, she always had to force herself to smile and act happy, so as not to anger her mother. Inside she was frightened, but her face said otherwise. Even if it was a lie. She reasoned, "If I don't smile right, she'll beat me." While drawing the mouth, the feeling reawakened, and it disturbed her. Her hands trembled, and she couldn't draw well. This same pain also arises in the drawing of the house next to the girl.' Again, she pointed at the picture.

'The house has no door. Without a door, you can't get inside, right? This house mirrors the girl's interior life. "No one is allowed inside." "I want to be alone in here." It illustrates her desire for a refuge from the outside world.

'Now, finally, I'd like you all to look at the drawing of the tree.

'The ends of the branches are sharp and pointed, like thorns. We sometimes see this pattern in drawings by criminals. It seems to express a defiant, aggressive nature. It says, "I will hurt you," or "I will prick you." Now, as a

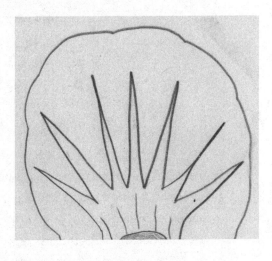

psychologist, I had to consider all this information together to diagnose the subject.'

Dr Hagio looked into the eyes of her students as she spoke, slowly and with careful deliberation.

'After looking at this picture, I concluded that Little A had a strong chance at rehabilitation. Can you see why? Look again at the tree. This time, look past the branches, and focus on the trunk. There is a little bird living in a hollow there.

People who draw pictures like this display a desire to protect, and a tendency towards strong nurturing love. It expresses the desire to defend the weak, and to create a safe haven for them to live in.

'Deep inside Little A's thorny, aggressive exterior beat a kind heart. If we gave her a chance to interact with animals or small children, we could foster that kindness and possibly overcome her aggressive spirit. That is what I surmised then, and, to this day, I remain confident in that diagnosis and recommended course of treatment. I understand that Little A is now living happily as a mother.'

CONTENTS

CHAPTER ONE

The Old Woman's Prayer

Shuhei Sasaki, May 19, 2014

In the window of an old apartment in a working-class Tokyo neighbourhood, a light glimmered despite the late hour.

The apartment's sole resident was twenty-one-year-old Shuhei Sasaki, a college student. He really should have been cramming for exams or working on a résumé for his upcoming job search, but that night he found himself glued to his computer screen for an altogether different reason.

'So, this must be the blog Kurihara was talking about,' he muttered to himself.

Kurihara was a younger student. He and Sasaki were both members of the college Paranormal Club. That afternoon, Sasaki had run into him in the cafeteria, and they had ended up having lunch together. Sasaki had been too busy with job hunting lately to attend any club meetings, so he was eager to catch up with his clubmate after so long away.

After they'd brought each other up to date and discussed the upcoming overnight with the club, naturally the talk turned to their shared interest in the bizarre and unexplained.

'So, Sasaki, have you gathered any intel lately?'

Kurihara wore an odd expression as he spoke. In their club, 'gathering intel' was code for watching or reading anything related to the paranormal.

'None. I've been swamped. I haven't seen any movies, read any books or even surfed online.'

'All right then, I'll put you onto something juicy. I just recently found a very strange blog.'

'A blog? What about?'

'It's called *Oh No, not Raku!* At first glance, it's perfectly innocent, but there's something there. Something *strange* about it. I can guarantee a chill, at the very least, so do give it a look.'

'Right . . .'

In Sasaki's experience, Kurihara was an easy-going kind of guy. He always preferred to hang back and stay out of things. So, when he recommended something with such enthusiasm, Sasaki knew he couldn't ignore it.

.   .   .

12 a.m. The only sound was the ticking of his clock. Sasaki gulped as he opened the blog Kurihara had told him about.

He felt . . . nostalgic, rather than nervous. Once, there had been so many blogs like this.

Ah, blogs. The concept now almost seemed quaint. Everyone had a different take on theirs. The blogs came in all sorts of styles: some simple diaries, some hobby sites, others outlets for political rants. . . . There was so much freedom to them, there had even been a time when you could find blogs 'written by' cats or rice

14

spatulas. But these past few years, the fever had died down, and you found far fewer than before.

By the title alone, you'd assume the author was named Raku, but it was such an unusual, suggestive name. A pen name? Probably.

And that exaggerated 'Oh no' was such a weak attempt at humor. The kind of uninspired silliness that was the hallmark of your average diary.

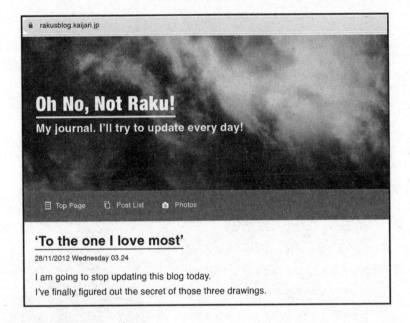

The latest post flickered beneath the title. It was dated November 28, 2012. So, about a year and a half ago. Meaning the blog hadn't been updated since.

It read:

'To the one I love most' 11/28/2012

I am going to stop updating this blog today.

I've finally figured out the secret of those three drawings.

I can't imagine the kind of pain you must have been suffering.

Nor can I understand the depths of whatever sin you committed.

I cannot forgive you. But even so, I will always love you.

Raku

Sasaki read this short, disturbing entry over and over. The more he did, the deeper the mystery grew.

He couldn't imagine what meaning lay behind the phrases 'To the one I love most', 'the secret of those three drawings' and 'whatever sin you committed'.

So he scrolled down, skimming past entries to see if they could help him unravel the mystery. The first entry was dated October 13, 2008. It read:

'Hello world!' 10/13/2008

I've decided to start keeping a blog from today. So, I guess I should begin by introducing myself. My name is Raku.

I was going to post a photo of myself, but while I was setting it up, I was told it's dangerous to post personal information on the web, so here's a drawing instead.

It's actually by my wife.

16

I'll just call her Yuki. She's six years older than me.

When I told her I was starting a blog, I asked if she would draw a picture of me to use instead of a photo, and it didn't even take her five minutes. That's what you get with a former pro illustrator! She's so talented!

But I think maybe she made me look too handsome. . . .

So, anyway, this is going to be like a diary, just me writing whatever I happen to feel like.

I plan to post every day, so I hope you keep reading!

Raku

'Anniversary' 10/15/2008

> *Hi there, it's Raku!*
>
> *I know I promised I'd update every day, but I was just so beat yesterday I went to bed without writing. Sorry. I'll do better from now on!*
>
> *So, today, October 15th, is a very important day.*
>
> *It's our first wedding anniversary!*
>
> *I bought a whole cake to celebrate. It was a little pricey, but so worth it!*
>
> *I ended up devouring two pieces, before Yuki scolded me, 'Don't eat so much! You'll get fat!' She's so mean! (SOB)*
>
> *The last four slices went into the fridge. That's tomorrow's breakfast. I can't wait!*

Raku

The entries went like that, four or five a week. They were all pretty tame, 'I ate so-and-so' or 'We went to do such-and-such', and Sasaki found no hint of anything that could be the 'sin' or 'pain' mentioned in the final entry.

Along the way, though, the couple's lives took a turn.

'Announcement' 12/25/2008
Hi there, it's Raku!
So, Yuki woke up feeling unwell, and it seems she went to hospital to get checked out this morning.
And, wouldn't you know it, they said she had a baby in there!
When Yuki told me, I was so happy I started jumping for joy! This is the best Christmas present ever!
So, I am hereby announcing that we are going to be a mummy and daddy!

Raku

From that point on, the blog was consumed by all things baby. Raku's entries overflowed with emotional writing about his expected child, as well as with concern for Yuki's condition.

'Morning sickness sucks' 1/3/2009
Yuki's morning sickness was really bad again today, so she could barely eat any of the New Year's leftovers.
All I can do is rub her back. I feel so powerless.
I've always heard that women start craving sour food when they have morning sickness, though I guess everyone's different.
Anyway, Yuki said she thought she could eat yogurt without feeling sick.
And so, our fridge is now packed with yogurt.
And I'm off to the store to buy more!

Raku

'Baby bump' 2/8/2009

Today we are entering the 13th week of pregnancy.

But it seems morning sickness isn't through with Yuki yet.

She ate a load of yogurt again today. She's tried a lot of different varieties, but it seems that the kind with aloe chunks agrees with her stomach best.

And speaking of her belly, she's really starting to show.

It's like I can see how the baby is growing! I'm so happy!

Raku

'Cherry blossoms' 3/16/2009

Yuki has started feeling a lot better, so today we went out for the first time in a while.

We went to the neighbourhood park. The cherry blossoms were beautiful, although they haven't reached full bloom yet.

We sat on a bench and talked about the baby.

Things like, 'What kinds of classes should we sign them up for when they're older?' and 'What anime should we watch with them first?'

We're rushing things a little, but imagining our lives with the baby is so much fun.

I want to start thinking up names, but we're going to wait until after we know if it's a boy or a girl before we do too much of that. Although, sitting under the cherry blossoms, we both agreed that Sakura would be a good name for a girl.

Raku

Up to that point, the couple's daily life had seemed one of endless sunshine.

But then, in May, when they'd passed the midpoint of Yuki's pregnancy, clouds appeared on the horizon.

'Ultrasound scan' 5/18/2009
I had the day off from work today, so I took Yuki to her pre-natal check-up.

It was so moving to get a first glimpse of the baby on the ultrasound!

But apparently it's a breech baby.

I've heard that breech babies can cause problems when it comes time to deliver, so that made me nervous. But the baby is still small, and I'm told they still move around a lot at this stage, so I was relieved to hear the doctor say it would probably turn itself the right way. Phew!

But there was another surprise to come.

Because the baby was head up, its pubic area was hidden behind Yuki's pelvic bone, so we still don't know if it's a boy or a girl.

So, I guess we'll have to pick a name without knowing!

Raku

A breech baby . . . that's what they call it when a baby is positioned head up and feet down in the mother's womb, the reverse of what usually happens. This discovery would go on to become a major issue for the couple.

'Doing our best!' 7/20/2009
We had another check-up.

The baby is still head up.

At this stage, apparently, it's very rare for babies to turn around on their own, so I guess we have to do it ourselves.

20

They taught us some exercises to help turn a breech baby.
Yuki is going to be doing them every day at home from now on.
  And I'll be there every step of the way, doing what I can to
support her!
  We're doing our best!

Raku

'Hot summer!' 8/18/2009
  We had another check-up today.
  We've both been working hard at the exercises, but the baby
is still the wrong way up.
  Yuki seems to be taking it pretty hard.
  But we were told that with proper preparation, she should be
able to deliver her breech baby normally. We're lucky we've got a
veteran midwife on hand!
  And so, it looks like we'll have to wait until the baby is born
to find out if it's a boy or a girl! (LOL)
  On the way home, we stopped by a cafe for juice.
  Yuki got a refill. Twice! We've been having so many hot days,
it's no wonder she's so thirsty lately.
  And since she's drinking for two, it must be hard to keep hydrated.

Raku

Then, on September 3rd, with the due date fast approaching,
something seemed to change in Yuki.

'Baby blues' 9/3/2009
  So, today Yuki suddenly broke down crying.
  She didn't answer when I asked why, so I was totally at a loss. . . .
  Maybe this is what they call 'baby blues'?

All I could do was sit there rubbing her back until she calmed down.

She could go into labour any time now, so I can't imagine how much stress she's feeling.

I really need to step up and be someone she can depend on. . . .

Raku

'Baby picture' 9/4/2009

Yuki has made a complete recovery from yesterday and is in high spirits!

And she also finally drew another picture!

It's adorable! She said she had imagined what our baby might look like.

When I asked her why it was dressed like Santa, she said, 'Because this baby is our Santa.'

It took me a while, but I finally clicked.

It's because we found out she was pregnant on Christmas Day! And it's already nine months later. . . . The time has gone by in a flash, but at the same time seems to have lasted forever. . . .

Raku

'Visions of the future' 9/5/2009

Yuki drew another picture today, like a sequel to yesterday's!

She said this time it's her idea of what the baby would look like when it's a little older.

She called it a 'vision of the future'.

Since the baby is still breech, we don't know what sex it will be, so she says she drew it ambiguously on purpose.

Talk about a pro! Most people would never pay attention to little details like that.

And I just noticed this, but I wonder what the number down at the bottom means. Yesterday's picture had one, too.

Yuki replied, 'It's a secret!' when I asked. . . . I keep thinking, but I just can't figure it out!

Raku

'The spitting image' 9/6/2009

We had soba noodles delivered for dinner tonight.

Mine had shrimp tempura. It was delicious!

So, Yuki drew another vision of the future for me today.

It's the baby all grown up!

Isn't it cool how her hair is blowing in the wind?

Yuki said that when she was drawing it, she was hoping that, if the baby's a girl, this is how she grows up to be.

She's the spitting image of Yuki herself! If she really does take after Yuki, she's going to be a beauty.

I guess she's going to draw the boy version tomorrow. I'm looking forward to it!

Raku

'The spitting image . . . ?' 9/7/2009

There are only three more days until the due date!

I'm worried about the delivery, but we are all so excited to meet the baby!

Now, on to today's vision of the future, the baby all grown up (boy version).

Yuki says, 'I made him look like his dad.'

No way, I'm not nearly that good-looking! But I'm happy she thinks so. . . .   Raku

'Prayer' 9/8/2009

Just two more days!

We're all ready, so everything will be fine no matter when contractions start.

Yuki seems nervous. But she still drew another picture!

She says that keeping her hands busy calms her down.

Today's vision of the future is a distant one. Apparently, it's supposed to be the baby as an old woman. She's dressed all in white, and praying, I guess?

When the baby is that age, I suppose the two of us will already be gone. . . .

But I shouldn't be such a downer! (LOL)

I bet tomorrow will be a granddad picture. I'm excited!

Raku

'Tomorrow's the day!' 9/9/2009

The due date is tomorrow.

I started getting all worked up this evening, but Yuki just laughed at me. 'Calm down,' she said.

Women really are so much stronger at times like this.

I guess she's all prepared.

But still, it looks like she wasn't in the mood to draw a picture today. I feel bad for expecting her to do one, actually. Sorry!

I imagine we're going to be pretty busy over the next few days, so I'm going to be taking a break from blogging.

I'm sure my next post will be a birth announcement!

Take care, everyone!

Raku

The next entry was posted about a month later.

'Announcement' 10/11/2009

So. It has been a while. This is Raku.

I have finally pulled myself together and am ready to let everyone know.

26

Yuki is gone.

The baby was born safely. Yuki's contractions started on the due date, and we rushed to the hospital.

Everything was going fine at first, but after a few hours of pushing, the baby wouldn't come. Then Yuki took a turn for the worse, and they had to perform an emergency caesarean.

They managed to save the baby, but Yuki passed away on the table.

The last month has flown by.

What with Yuki's funeral and taking care of the baby, I haven't really had time to grieve.

But sitting here, alone, writing this, the tears are falling.

It's hard, but I have to be strong for my baby.

I will do my best to raise our child.

Raku

Sasaki sat, stunned, staring at the screen. His heart was overflowing with emotions, but he had no way to deal with them. Yuki and Raku were, of course, complete strangers to him. He'd only started reading this blog out of curiosity.

But as he was scrolling through the entries, at some point he'd found himself emotionally involved. And now he was feeling a kind of loss he'd never experienced before.

What kind of life awaited them, the father and child left behind?

Sasaki couldn't help wondering about their futures. He was desperate to see Raku carry on after Yuki's death and find happiness raising their child.

With that prayer in his heart, he clicked the 'Read next entry' link.

The page appeared.

When he saw the title, Sasaki blinked in disbelief.

'To the one I love most' 11/28/2012

I am going to stop updating this blog today.

I've finally figured out the secret of those three drawings.

I can't imagine the kind of pain you must have been suffering.

Nor can I understand the depths of whatever sin you committed.

I cannot forgive you. But even so, I will always love you.

Raku

That was the very first entry he'd read.

In other words, after the announcement of his wife's death on October 11th 2009, Raku hadn't posted for three years, until he suddenly broke his silence with this entry. Sasaki read it once more.

'The one I love most . . .' That must mean Yuki. You would think, then, that the post was addressed to his deceased wife.

'Whatever sin you committed . . .' There was nothing in the blog hinting at Yuki committing any transgression.

'I cannot forgive you.' What could his beloved wife have done that he couldn't forgive?

'The secret of those three drawings . . .' These must be the 'visions of the future' that Yuki had drawn as her due date approached.

So, a talented artist drew some pictures of her unborn child's imagined future. It was an unusual thing to do, perhaps, but not particularly odd. Sasaki could only believe that, as she drew

them, Yuki was full of hope that her child would live a long, healthy life.

But Raku had looked at three of those five drawings and discovered some hidden secret. What could it possibly be? Sasaki had the feeling he was standing clueless before some kind of maddeningly difficult puzzle.

But it wasn't that he didn't have any hints. There were those numbers written in the margins of the pictures.

Each of the five drawings had its own number somewhere. When Raku asked what they meant, Yuki had dodged the question, saying, 'It's a secret!' They seemed like the key to the whole thing.

Sasaki turned on his printer and printed out the drawings. He arranged them sequentially: (1) Baby, (2) Old woman, (3) Adult (woman), (4) Child, (5) Adult (man), but the chronology was all mixed up.

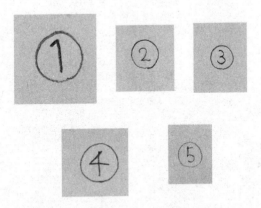

'It starts with the baby . . . Skips to old woman, then back to child . . . And adult again? That doesn't make any sense. . . .'

Sasaki sighed and lay down on the floor. He looked out the window and saw the sky was already lightening. It would soon be dawn.

'I have to get a bit of sleep. . . .'

He decided to squeeze in a nap before his ten-thirty lecture.

.   .   .

The student cafeteria was always packed after twelve. If you wanted to grab a seat, you had to make it in while the hour hand still hovered in 'eleven' territory. Sasaki slid out of his morning lecture just a tad early and ran for the cafeteria.

He wasn't after lunch, though. He was after Kurihara.

The rush paid off, and the tables were still empty. He looked around for Kurihara but . . . No luck. It seemed he wasn't there yet.

As Sasaki was thinking he should go ahead and get his lunch ticket, someone slapped him on the shoulder.

'Sasaki! We meet again. I saw you tearing across the campus just now. Are you starving, or what?'

It was Kurihara.

The two picked up plates of rice and curry, then sat across from each other at a table.

'Hey, Kurihara, I read that blog you told me about.'

'It's quite the puzzler, right?'

'It really is. I barely got any sleep last night. I keep thinking about it, but I can't figure it out. It's so weird.'

'I know!'

'I mean, if it wasn't for that last entry, it would be a fairly common, if tragic, domestic story.'

'Would it?' Kurihara asked, and his eyes flashed. Sasaki couldn't help but flinch.

'Sasaki . . . I agree that the last entry is creepy, true enough. But that's hardly the only creepy thing. There's something off about the whole story.'

'What are you talking about?'

'Well, for example . . . The entries after the birth were all deleted.'

'Wait, what was deleted?'

'You can tell by reading the last entry. Hold on a minute.'

Kurihara opened his bag and took out a bundle of stapled sheets of A4 paper. He put the bundle on the table, and Sasaki saw it was a printout of the blog.

'Wait, Kurihara . . . Did you seriously print out the whole blog?'

'Of course! I wanted to be able to read it on the way to school so I could figure it out.'

'To the one I love most' 11/18/2012

> I am going to stop updating this blog today.
> I've finally figured out the secret of those three drawings.
> I can't imagine the kind of pain you must have been suffering.
> Nor can I understand the depths of whatever sin you committed.
> I cannot forgive you. But even so, I will always love you.
>
> Raku

'So, it says, "I am going to stop updating this blog today." This is the crucial line. Usually, when a person swears to "stop doing X today," it's understood that the action has, until now, been habitual. Like, if someone announces, "Today, I'm quitting smoking," it's obvious that they had been smoking up to the day before. So, in the same way, the line "I am going to stop updating this blog today" implies that Raku had been updating the blog fairly regularly up to this point.'

'But, from the entry before— the one where he announces that

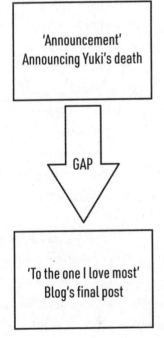

'Announcement'
Announcing Yuki's death

GAP

'To the one I love most'
Blog's final post

Yuki died, right?—from there to this entry there's a gap of almost three years that's unaccounted for. That got me thinking. I bet Raku kept updating the blog regularly during those years. But then he must have deleted all of those entries, for some reason.'

'Hmm . . .'

'Deleting a blog isn't that unusual. I mean, I deleted my *Evangelion* analysis blog I kept back in middle school. But the way Raku did it is a little odd. He left the entries from when his wife was alive but deleted the ones about his child. . . . There's something kind of off there. I can't figure out his motive.'

'Now that you say it, there is something strange about it . . . And it went right over my head.'

'There are other weird things, too. Here, read the entry for October 15th.'

'Anniversary' 10/15/2008

Hi there, it's Raku!

I know I promised I'd update every day, but I was just so beat yesterday I went to bed without writing. Sorry. I'll do better from now on!

So, today, October 15th, is a very important day.

It's our first wedding anniversary!

I bought a whole cake to celebrate. It was a little pricey, but so worth it!

I ended up devouring two pieces before Yuki scolded me, "Don't eat so much! You'll get fat!' She's so mean! (SOB)

The last four slices went into the fridge. That's tomorrow's breakfast. I can't wait!

Raku

'All right, Sasaki, here's a pop quiz for you. How many pieces of cake did Yuki eat?'

'Um . . . She went after Raku for eating too much when he had two, so it's safe to assume she only ate one, right?'

'Right. If she'd had two, Raku could have shot back, "You're one to talk!" And so, that day, Yuki had one piece, and Raku had two. He said there were four slices left over, making a total of seven. Which would mean they served a cake cut into seven pieces. Isn't that weird?'

'Yeah, it is. Most people would divide a round cake like that evenly.'

'Exactly. I think it's safe to assume that the cake that day was cut into eight pieces. Yuki had one, Raku had two and there were four left over. That makes seven. . . . So, what do you think happened to the other one?'

'Uh . . .'

'Someone else must have eaten it. Haven't you sensed that someone else, besides the two of them, is living in that house?'

'What?! Come on, aren't you reading too much into this? Like, Raku probably just wrote the wrong number somewhere.'

'This isn't an unfounded assumption, of course. You can catch hints of this unseen third person in other entries. Let's go back to the very first one.'

'Hello world!' 10/13/2008

I've decided to start keeping a blog from today. So, I guess I should begin by introducing myself. My name is Raku.

I was going to post a photo of myself, but while I was setting it up, I was told it's dangerous to post personal information on the web, so here's a drawing instead.

It's actually by my wife.

I'll just call her Yuki. She's six years older than me.

When I told her I was starting a blog, I asked if she would draw a picture of me to use instead of a photo, and it didn't even take her five minutes. That's what you get with a former pro illustrator! She's so talented!

But I think maybe she made me look too handsome. . . .

So, anyway, this is going to be like a diary, just me writing whatever I happen to feel like.

I plan to post every day, so I hope you keep reading!

Raku

'At the top, he writes: "I was told it's dangerous to post personal information on the web." So, who do you think told Raku that?'

'Yuki did, right?'

'You'd think that, right? But then, look at this line.'

When I told her I was starting a blog, I asked if she would draw a picture of me to use instead of a photo, and it didn't even take her five minutes.

'He tells her specifically that he has started a blog, so I think we can confidently say that before this point in time, Yuki was unaware.'

Raku decides to start a blog

He is told it's dangerous to post personal information

Raku informs Yuki that he is starting a blog

'So, then the question arises, who warned Raku about sharing personal information online? There's a distinct possibility that someone else is living with them. One of their parents, a sibling, a friend . . . I don't know who, but what I do know is that Raku is hiding their existence. Their name doesn't appear once in the blog. But still, here and there, you got a sense of their impact on Raku and Yuki's lives. I wonder what's behind all the secrecy. . . .'

Sasaki began to feel a nameless fear take hold as Kurihara went on.

'Of course, that's just the beginning.'

'Wait, there's more?'

'Yes. The thing that really got me scared was the part about the breech baby.'

But we were told that with proper preparation, she should be able to deliver her breech baby normally. We're lucky we've got a veteran midwife on hand!

'Reading that literally gave me a chill. I have a younger sister who was a breech baby, so I'm vaguely familiar with the risks involved, and breech births are almost always very difficult. I believe that in the days before people understood the condition, lots of mothers and babies died. Nowadays, though, once they know that it will be a breech birth, hospitals immediately schedule a caesarean. Of course, there are always exceptions, but there is no way a responsible doctor would say, "With proper preparation, you should be able to deliver a breech baby normally." And Yuki did actually die in childbirth.'

'So, they got a bogus doctor?'

'Yeah. Everything going on around Yuki was bizarre, what

with this mysterious housemate and Raku's attempts to hide them, and the terrible hospital they found.'

. . .

'By the way, Kurihara, what do you think of those pictures?'

'You mean the "secret of those three drawings" stuff?'

'Right. I tried all kinds of things, but I couldn't figure it out,' Sasaki said.

'Did you look at the numbers scattered around?'

'Of course.'

'Those numbers are right at the heart of it.'

'Yeah, I thought so, too. But, when I arranged the pictures in numerical order, the timeline got all messed up. I got nothing from them.'

'Sasaki, numbering things can indicate more than just chronological order.'

'What are you talking about?'

'What I mean is, maybe the timeline isn't what you should be worried about.'

'Kurihara . . . Are you telling me you've figured out what the pictures mean?!'

Kurihara flashed a toothy grin. 'Well, I think I have.'

'You have?! Tell me!'

'Um . . . It might be a little tricky here. I don't have the right tools.'

'You need tools?'

'Could you drop by the club room today? I could show you there.'

'The club? Well . . . I haven't shown my face in a while. I'm not sure I'd be welcome.'

'Come on, Sasaki, you're a member! You're always welcome!'

'Really?'

'Of course.'

'All right then. I'll stop by later. It'll be a good break from job hunting.'

Kurihara grinned when he heard that. 'Woohoo! I've been lonely without you, Sasaki!'

'I never pegged you as the type to feel lonely. Anyway, I've got class after this, so it'll probably be around four when I get there.'

'That's fine. Oh, right. Here, you take this.'

Kurihara handed Sasaki the bundle of printed blog entries.

'Are you sure? Weren't you going to solve the mystery on your commute?'

'It's fine. I've got a few spares.'

'You're obsessed. . . . Fine, then, I'll take it. Thanks.'

'No problem. Right. I'll be waiting in the club room. Just, keep this in mind: the numbers are at the centre of it all.'

.   .   .

All through his third class, Sasaki stared at the booklet Kurihara had given him. The professor was notorious for rambling on endlessly, so lots of students—not just Sasaki— tuned out, using the period as free time for catching up on schoolwork or sleep.

Even so, it wasn't as if he were wearing earplugs, so he could still hear the professor drone on in the background.

'. . . is a good example of how art and architecture are closely connected. That applies to painting, as well, and as everyone knows, Maurits Escher, who became famous for the optical illusions in his work, studied architecture at university in Haarlem. . . .'

Optical illusions . . .

The words sparked something in Sasaki's mind.

Could Yuki's 'visions of the future' also be some kind of trick?

Sasaki was no art expert, but he'd seen plenty of strange pictures that tricked the eye, like the one that looked like a rabbit from one angle and a duck from another, or the picture that looked like a skull from afar but human twins up close. They all shared a common thread in that they looked completely different based on perspective.

I've finally figured out the secret of those three drawings.

Years after Yuki's death, could Raku have found a different perspective on her drawings?

Sasaki leafed through the booklet and studied the 'visions of the future'. He tried spinning the drawings around and noticed something.

When he rotated the picture of the woman ninety degrees, rather than standing with her hair blowing in the wind, it looked like she was lying on her back with her hair draped down. For an instant he felt like he'd made a breakthrough, but his enthusiasm quickly faded. What difference did it make if she was standing or lying down? On top of that, the position of her arm looked unnaturally stiff.

Just then, the classroom filled with noise. The students were getting ready to leave. It seemed the professor had concluded his lecture without him noticing. One student opened the classroom door. A strong breeze blew in from the hallway, and the booklet in his hand fluttered in the wind.

The sight lit another spark in Sasaki's brain.

Page one, page two, page three . . .

'*Sasaki, numbering things can indicate more than just chronological order . . .*'

Could they actually be layers? Maybe the pictures were supposed to be laid on top of each other?

If you did so, and arranged the pictures in the right way, maybe they'd resemble something completely different, like an illusion.

Sasaki tore the drawing pages from the booklet and tried layering them in order: (1) Baby, (2) Old woman, (3) Woman. Then, he held them up to the light.

The three pictures blended together, but they didn't seem to reveal anything in particular.

He tried adjusting the pictures, changing the angles, changing their positions. . . . He tried all kinds of things, but eventually just slumped back in his chair in despair. There were endless possible configurations.

'Damn. If only I had some kind of hint . . .'

Then, Kurihara's words came back to him.

'*Those numbers are right at the heart of it.*'

'*Just, remember this: the numbers are at the centre of it all.*'

He didn't need to be told that the numbers were the key to solving the puzzle. . . . Why was he so insistent about something so obvious, to the point of repeating it like that?

'No, wait a minute . . . Could "centre" actually mean . . . ?'

Sasaki thought about it. In this case, 'centre' might mean exactly that.

The focus. The core. The axis point where several things connected . . . Like the staple holding together his bundled booklet.

Sasaki arranged the pictures again, with the numbers 1, 2, and 3 in the same location. Keeping the numbers at the centre, he rotated the three pictures. He was hoping that the three drawings might fall into place and create a wholly new picture.

But the only result was failure.

.　　.　　.

At four that afternoon, Sasaki promptly stepped into the club building, which stood by itself in a distant corner of the campus.

It was packed with rooms used by all kinds of cultural and literary clubs. It had been half a year since he had last opened the door to the Paranormal Club. Inside the small space, packed with books and magazines, Kurihara sat reading alone.

'Sorry it took so long. Where are the others?'

'These days, it's usually just me.'

Sasaki realized that the club was dying out. It had always been small, and now the students in Sasaki's year were all getting ready for graduation and finding jobs. He felt a little sorry for Kurihara.

'Right then, Sasaki. Ready for the secret of the—'

'Hold on a second. I was actually just making my own deductions earlier.'

Sasaki shared the inspirations he'd had during class about optical illusions and the 'centre'.

Kurihara nodded along. 'I see. You're onto a pretty good line of reasoning there. I think that's near enough to call it right.'

'How so? I haven't solved the puzzle yet.'

'You're on the right track, you just need to take one more step. Listen, Sasaki, this is a puzzle. Those five drawings are the pieces you need to assemble. Now, let's imagine. If the pieces of a jigsaw puzzle were all different sizes, could you put it together?'

'You don't mean . . .'

'Those five drawings were all originally done on paper. Then, Raku took photos of them or something and uploaded them to his blog. The important part is you can't tell the original size of the drawings by looking at the photos.'

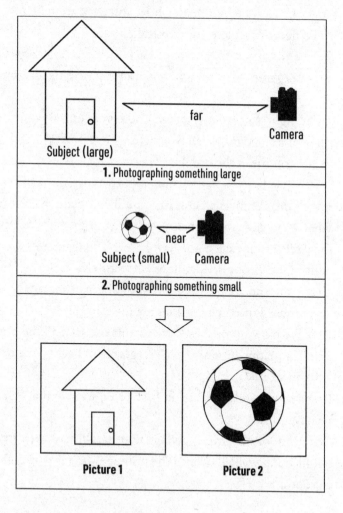

far

Camera

Subject (large)

1. Photographing something large

near

Subject (small)   Camera

2. Photographing something small

Picture 1   Picture 2

'For example, when you take a photo of something big, you have to step back to get everything into frame. And, with something small, you do the opposite and get closer. The result is that the objects in the pictures all look the same size.'

'If the sheets of paper Yuki used for the drawings were all different sizes, we wouldn't be able to tell by the pictures. In other words, after they were scanned, the pieces of our puzzle would no longer be to scale. No matter how you tried to match them up, you'd never complete your optical illusion.'

"So, we just need to get them back to their original sizes? But we can't know what they were without seeing the originals, right?'

'You're right, but we can guess. There is a central point that can serve as a standard for all five pictures.'

'Cen— You mean the numbers?'

'Exactly. Just like you figured out, if you arrange the pictures in order with the numbers all lined up, you'll complete the picture. But what we need to focus on now isn't the numbers themselves, but the circle around each one. Look, see? The diameters are all different, right? If our deduction is correct—that is, if the numbers really are the centre—then it would be natural to assume that she drew all those circles roughly the same size.'

'So, if we blow up or shrink the pictures so that all the numbers' circles are the same size, we can get them back to the original relative sizes?'

'That's right. And I asked you here to do exactly that. Here, let me have those.'

Kurihara took the five drawings that Sasaki had torn from the booklet and walked over to the printer sitting in one corner of the room.

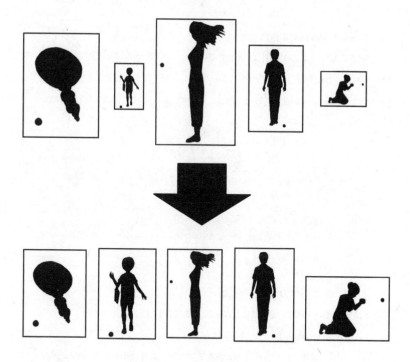

'Let's see . . . We'll blow up this one twenty per cent . . . And shrink this one ten per cent . . . And this one . . .'

Muttering to himself, he deftly manipulated the controls, until the printer spat out five drawings.

'All done. I think we've got the original relative sizes now.'

'They're so different . . . All right, then, let's line them up.'

'Hold on there. You've got one more major problem, Sasaki.'

'I do?'

'You said earlier that you layered them and held them up to the light, right?'

'Right.'

'So, listen. We've got five drawings numbered one to five. Those numbers should indicate the order of the pictures. And that should also mean that, if the order is wrong, the trick won't work.'

'Yeah, I suppose so.'

'Now, if you hold them up to the light, what difference does the order make? Basically, 123, 231, 321, it doesn't matter. The picture will always be the same. They all just blend together.'

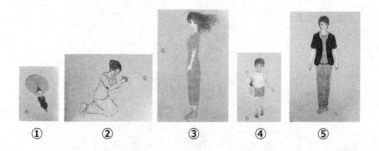

①   ②   ③   ④   ⑤

'Then, what should we do?'

'Have you ever heard of layer composition before?'

'No, sorry, never heard of it.'

'It's a common technique for illustrators. So, let's say an artist gets a commission, say to "draw a picture of a boy holding a rice ball against a backdrop of some hills".'

'But lots of times clients tweak their requests after the picture is done. Like, "Let's change the rice ball to a sandwich," or "Change the boy to a girl," or "Change the background from a hillside to a cityscape." If they had to redraw the whole picture for each change, they'd never be able to keep up. So, instead, they divide the picture into "layers" as they draw.'

46

'First, they make the background layer of the Hills (1). Next is the Boy (2), and last comes the Rice Ball (3).

'Removing the negative space around each drawing, they stack the layers 1, 2, and 3 to complete the picture. Then, if the client decides to skimp on the rice ball, all they have to do is redraw layer 3. But one thing to be careful about is the order of the layers. If you reverse 2 and 3, for example, the rice ball will end up hidden behind the boy. So, order is super important in layer composition. The blog said that Yuki had been a professional illustrator, so I think layer composition would have been second nature. In which case . . .'

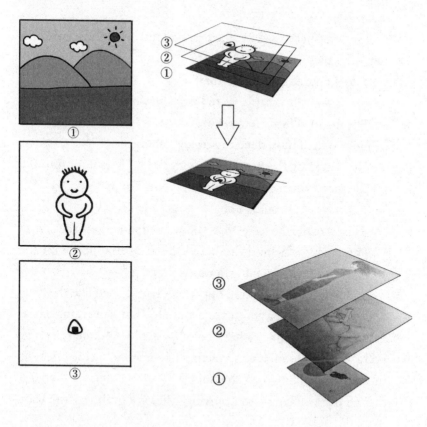

'The drawing labelled 1, the baby, is our background, the bottom layer. Layer 2, the old woman, goes on top of that, and then last, we have 3, the adult woman. Let's try it with those three.'

Kurihara stacked the three layers so that the circled numbers aligned, then he adjusted the three pictures around the numbers.

'Here . . . I think.'

'Did it work?'

'I hope so. We need to cut away the negative space, though.'

Kurihara fetched some scissors and started cutting.

As he did so, Sasaki started to see it. A picture was taking form. A sickening one. Meanwhile, Kurihara hummed happily away as he cut.

'Hey, Kurihara,' Sasaki asked, in a fearful voice. 'Do you know what this picture will reveal?'

'I do. I figured it out yesterday.'

'So . . . Why do you seem to be having so much fun?'

'Because it is fun. Here we are!'

He laid the finished picture on the table.

The secret of those three drawings . . . The solution to the puzzle that Yuki had hidden within them. There it was.

'No way . . . It couldn't be.'

'This has to be the secret that Yuki wanted someone to decipher.'

The cushion behind the baby's head overlapped with the woman's stomach, making her look pregnant.

And when Sasaki figured out why it had looked like the baby was 'dressed like Santa' he felt a chill. That red triangle was actually a gash in its mother's belly, wasn't it? And the red on its body was her blood. It was a picture of someone slicing open the mother and pulling the baby out.

The old woman wasn't praying. She was grabbing the baby

and pulling it from its mother's body. Those white clothes weren't some religious outfit, they were doctor's scrubs.

And then he looked at the woman's body. The pale skin. The expressionless face, the staring eyes. The unnaturally stiff arms.

It was a picture of a corpse, wasn't it?

'You don't mean to say, this picture . . . ?'

'That's right.'

They managed to save the baby, but Yuki passed away on the table.

'It's just as he wrote in the blog entry. The baby was surgically delivered, meaning by c-section, and she died on the operating table.'

'So, they cut open her belly and removed the baby. Like the picture shows.'

Hiding someone's real fate in a trick picture like this would ordinarily be perverse. . . . But this was different. Yuki had drawn this before she died.

Yuki had secretly drawn a picture of her own death.

Those words, 'visions of the future . . .' They lay heavy on his heart.

'Yuki predicted her own death?' he asked Kurihara.

'You think she had the power of precognition?'

'I mean, if not, how would you explain it?'

'Well, it could have been that she knew someone was going to kill her.' Kurihara was matter-of-fact.

'What?!'

'Just, you know, for example. Like, what if someone on the obstetrics staff held a grudge against her and had planned to kill her during delivery?'

'Oh, come on, that's a bit far-fetched.'

'Would you say it's an unreasonable hypothesis? Remember,

it was someone at the hospital who gave that crazy recommendation to deliver a breech baby normally.'

'But we were told that with proper preparation, she should be able to deliver her breech baby normally.'

'The result of that was that Yuki had trouble in delivery, and she died. You could almost say that her death was murder planned by the hospital.'

'Someone at the hospital intended to murder her?!'

Kurihara nodded. 'And then, one day, Yuki figured out the plan. So, these drawings were her way of letting Raku know that she might die during childbirth.'

'Let's say for the sake of argument that's true. Why go to all this trouble of hiding that truth in some innocent pictures? Why not just tell Raku?' Sasaki asked.

'There must have been something keeping her from talking to him. If what Raku wrote in his blog was true, then Yuki must have committed some kind of sin in the past. And he implies it was something truly terrible.'

Nor can I understand the depths of whatever sin you committed.

'So, the reason someone at the hospital wanted to kill Yuki was revenge for that sin?' Sasaki was still confused.

'If that were the case, then talking to Raku about it would mean confessing.'

I cannot forgive you. But even so, I will always love you.

'"I cannot forgive you . . ." That implies that whatever Yuki did, it had something to do with Raku. And that's why she couldn't tell him. It might even be that she was ready to accept death out of remorse for whatever it was. But she wanted Raku to know the truth after her death, so she left him a coded message.'

'How awful.'

51

'Well, this is all just speculation on my part. Don't take it too seriously.'

'No, I think you're—'

'It doesn't really matter how much we think about it, anyway, because we'll never know the truth. In the end, to them, we're still just a couple of strangers. No connection at all.'

.　　.　　.

Afterwards, the two went out, having dinner at a little diner near campus, before going their separate ways. As they parted, Kurihara said, 'Sasaki, sorry for taking up so much of your time today. I know you're busy.'

'Don't worry about it. I enjoyed getting back into the club again. Thanks.'

'No—thank you. Are you back to the job hunt again tomorrow?'

'Yeah. Two different companies are having information sessions tomorrow, then I have class after.'

'It sounds rough. I think I'm going to keep working out some ideas about that blog.'

'Well, if you figure out the truth, let me know.'

'I will. Promise.'

On the way home, Sasaki tried to break down Kurihara's reasoning.

- In the past, Yuki committed some mortal sin.
- Some member of staff in the hospital Ob/Gyn department held a grudge against her over that, and recommended a hazardous birth plan as an indirect means of killing Yuki.

52

- Yuki figured out the plan, and drew that trick picture as a dying message.
- Unaware, Raku happily posted the drawings on his blog.
- Then, Yuki died during childbirth.
- A few years after Yuki's death, Raku figured out the secret of the pictures, and in doing so grasped both the truth of her death and the sin she committed.

It all seemed so far-fetched.

In the first place, he couldn't figure out why she'd go to a hospital where someone who hated her so much was working. And if she figured out there was a plan to kill her, she'd just go to the police, right? She could always change hospitals, couldn't she? Why didn't Yuki try to get help?

All she did was draw trick pictures.

'Pictures . . . Hey, wait a minute . . .' Sasaki suddenly felt he had caught onto something big.

Kurihara had figured out the secret of the three pictures. But there were actually five pictures. What was the reason for those other two? Wasn't it likely there was some trick to them, too?

Sasaki took out the remaining two pictures that Kurihara had adjusted for size on his printer, (4) Child and (5) Man. He stacked the two pictures with the numbers aligned. When he did, his heart gave a painful lurch.

'Oh, this is . . .'

There was no need to cut away the white space. He held up the pictures so that the street light shone through from behind.

It was a father and child, walking hand in hand.

Another vision of the future . . .

Yuki had drawn a picture of the future after she was gone. What had she been feeling as she did so?

Sasaki suddenly wanted to talk to Kurihara again. He wanted to know what the man thought.

He turned around and began running the way he had come. Kurihara couldn't have gone far.

But, no matter where he looked, he could not find Kurihara.

CHAPTER TWO

The Smudged Room

Yuta Konno

Yuta Konno's father Haruto died during the winter, three years ago.

Yuta was only three years old at the time, so he didn't really understand what had happened. He hadn't cried or been sad. But the sight of his mama, always so quiet and gentle, totally overcome with grief made him feel that something very bad must have happened. It filled him with anxiety and fear.

Now, Yuta was almost six. The few hazy memories he had of his father were fading away, bit by bit. But one memory remained clear.

It was three summers ago, just a few months before his father's death. His father had taken Yuta to the cemetery to pray. It was just a ten minute walk from home. Yuta, wearing a wide straw hat under the brilliant blue sky, listened as his father spoke in his kind voice.

But try as he might, Yuta could never remember what he had said.

All he could hear in his mind was the thunderous chorus of the cicadas.

Naomi Konno was in a sour mood as she prepared dinner. She peeled a thick scallion and chopped it finely, but the whole time her attention was directed at the next room. The living room was quiet. Yuta was probably sprawled on the sofa, on the verge of tears. She put the frying pan on the stove and added oil. In went the scallions, and she began stir-frying. Her head spun with thoughts.

I was too hard on him.

But it's an important lesson.

But surely there must have been another way to say it?

But there are things you can't teach with kind words.

The scallions softened and a sweet aroma filled the air. Grabbing some mince from the fridge, she added it to the pan.

Yuta liked to draw. When he was very little, he would sit and happily draw squiggly lines for hours, but now he had graduated on to people, animals and vehicles. He could draw proper pictures. He had even started using tools to help. Right now, his favorite was a stencil ruler.

It was a large plastic ruler with holes in it of different shapes: circles, triangles, stars. Even a small child could draw perfect shapes by tracing the inside of those holes with a pen or pencil. And it seemed to be so, so much fun. Which was fine, of course. He was welcome to draw all he wanted, provided it was on his drawing paper.

But on the linoleum? In permanent marker? And this wasn't the first time either. Earlier he had drawn on the bathroom wall. And before that it was the pillar in the living room. She had scrubbed and scrubbed, but they had only faded a little, not disappeared.

'Children are filled with infinite curiosity. Drawing on things is an important means of self-expression. It is silly to scold them for it.' She had read that in a child-rearing article once. The author was clearly a homeowner.

'I wonder if they'd say the same thing if they were a renter?' Naomi had muttered bitterly to herself.

When she saw that the meat had browned, she took a block of tofu and cut it into cubes in her hand. Those, too, went in. A great sizzling came from the pan. She opened the box of mapo tofu mix, took out a packet of mild paste, and added it as well. Naomi liked spicy food. When she was younger, she hadn't even considered food without spice worthy of human consumption, but becoming a mother had opened her eyes to the pleasures of milder, sweeter sauces. Just as the mapo tofu started bubbling in earnest, the rice maker played its song, indicating the rice was ready.

Naomi gave a sigh and forced a smile, trying to change her mood. She headed to the living room.

'Yuta dear, dinner's ready.'

From where he sat, Yuta eyed Naomi cautiously, trying to read her expression. Was Mama feeling better, or still angry?

I did the same when I was a child and my parents got angry at me.

Naomi intentionally made her voice gentler as she said, 'Mama's not mad any more. Come on, let's eat.' She smiled.

'OK. I'll eat.'

The tension in Yuta's expression eased a little.

. . .

After dinner was over and Yuta was bathed and put to bed, Naomi washed the dishes, folded the laundry and was finally able to rest. It was eleven o'clock. The day's exhaustion washed over her as she sunk into the sofa. *I'm not so young any more. Can I really raise this boy on my own?* She wasn't making enough from her part-time job to save any money. Their apartment was one of the cheapest in the city, but she still struggled to make rent every month.

School, exams, job hunting . . . How would she find the money for all the stages of life ahead of Yuta? Could she keep him safe that whole time?

It felt like she was running a marathon with no finish line.

And it wasn't only the future that scared her. There was something else weighing on her mind lately.

Someone is following me.

She first had the feeling two days earlier, in the evening. On the way home, after she had finished work and picked up Yuta from nursery school, she had suddenly sensed someone watching them from behind. But when she turned around, no one was there. It must have been her imagination.

But the next day, she once again felt the unsettling presence of someone behind them on the way home.

Then today, she finally confirmed her suspicions. They had stopped by a convenience store on the way home to do some shopping. When they stepped out, a compact car in front of the shop caught her eye. It stood out to her; it wasn't a model she'd seen around the neighborhood.

When they resumed walking again, the car began to slowly move, trailing them. Her nerves tightened. The car kept moving, maintaining a fixed distance behind them. The driver was clearly acting oddly. Should they run away? Should they stop? Turn around? Every option she considered had its dangers, so instead she just gripped Yuta's hand tightly and kept walking.

Soon, their apartment building came into view.

'Come on, Yuta, let's hurry!'

Naomi pulled Yuta by the hand and quickened her pace. They burst into the building's entrance, and just after they had, the car sped up and drove past. It confirmed her worst fears.

'Oh, if only Haruto were still here,' Naomi muttered to herself, staring at the family Buddhist altar in one corner of the room. It was a vain wish, but one she couldn't help making every evening. Yuta's father, Haruto, smiled from the framed picture on the altar.

Naomi slowly lifted herself from the sofa. She took the small bowl of mapo tofu from its place of offering on the altar, covered it in plastic wrap and put it away in the fridge. That would be her breakfast. She went back to the living room, offered a brief prayer before the picture, then finally headed for bed.

Yuta was deeply asleep in his own futon laid out beside hers. He was probably exhausted from all his crying. Yuta was looking more and more like Haruto lately. She wanted him to grow up like Haruto had, as well. With that prayer in her heart, she slipped into her futon.

.   .   .

'Listen, I shop here all the time, all right? So, you know, if you can't offer me any better customer service than that, then maybe I'll just take my business elsewhere. Do you hear me?'

The old woman had been spouting similar threats for a good

five minutes. She appeared dissatisfied with the way Naomi had bagged her groceries and was haranguing her about it.

'I think you need to go back and learn how to treat customers again. From the start. Let me see your name tag. Konno, is it? I'll make sure to let your boss know about this. Oh, you have just put me in the worst mood!'

After spitting out that final complaint, she walked away, still emanating rage. Naomi saw her off, standing in a deep bow. She sneaked a glance at the clock on her register. It was already past six, when she should have clocked out.

She punched her timecard, quickly changed out of her uniform and rushed out of the shop. Yuta's nursery school would look after the children until seven in the evening. But even so, nearly all the children were picked up soon after six. Anyone staying later ended up waiting for their parents alone with the teacher. Naomi had seen that lonely sight more times than she cared to. She desperately wanted to spare Yuta any more loneliness, son of a single parent as he was. That thought drove Naomi as she ran through the streets.

She arrived just before 6:15.

When she stepped through the nursery gate, a high-pitched voice exclaimed, 'Oh! It's Yuta's mama!' A girl in braids and a large, bearded man came walking towards the gate. It was a classmate of Yuta's, Miu Yonezawa, and her father. Miu was a particularly good friend of Yuta's. Naomi crouched a little and said, 'Hello, Miu!' with a smile. Then she straightened up to greet the girl's father.

'Good evening, Mr Yonezawa.'

'And a good evening to you, Mrs Konno. Another hard day for both of us, I suppose.'

'Yes, same as always.'

'Of course. Next month, we're planning a little barbecue at the house. We'd love to have you and Yuta over to play! We'll have more beef than we can eat. The best Yonezawa beef, you know!'

'Pardon?'

'Oh, just a little joke, you know how there's a beef called Yonezawa. And since our last name is Yonezawa . . . well, anyways, any beef we buy becomes Yonezawa beef. . . . Just a little joke.'

'Daddy, you're bombing!' Miu chimed unhappily. Her perfect timing sent Naomi into peals of laughter.

'There I go again . . . Miu, you're such a harsh critic!'

Daddy Yonezawa smiled, if a little embarrassedly, then walked off happily hand in hand with his daughter. Naomi stared after them, her heart warmed.

Mrs Yonezawa was currently in the hospital with cancer. At the end of the month, though, she would be returning home for hospice care. Every family had their cross to bear, it seemed.

Even in difficult times, everyone is staying so positive. I have to try hard, too. Naomi felt buoyed up, somehow.

Inside, Yuta and his group's teacher, Miho Haruoka, were working on a jigsaw puzzle together. Naomi saw that, once again, he was the last child to be picked up.

'Yuta, I'm sorry I'm late!' she said. Yuta glanced up, then looked back down at the puzzle.

'Wait a minute, Mama, I'm not done with the puzzle.' This curt tone didn't suit his child's voice. He had stopped running to her with a glad 'Mama!' when he was around four and a half. It seemed he had already decided it was 'uncool' to appear too clingy to his mama in public. It was a little sad for Naomi, but perhaps it was better that way for boys.

Ms Haruoka chided Yuta as he stared at the puzzle, then said, 'Yuta, there's something I want to talk to Mama about. Can you wait here alone for a minute?'

Naomi's heart skipped a beat. Had something happened?

Yuta looked displeased, but Ms Haruoka placated him, saying, 'Show me the finished puzzle when I get back, all right? I'm looking forward to it!'

It must have worked, because Yuta nodded and attacked the puzzle with newfound determination.

Ms Haruoka guided Naomi to the staffroom.

'I'm sorry to bother you when I know you must be tired. Please, have a seat,' she said.

'Thank you.'

Naomi sank into a folding chair as Ms Haruoka brought another one over and sat next to her.

'Has anything changed recently with Yuta at home?'

'Changed? What do you mean?'

'For example . . . Has he started watching any scary TV programmes or anything?'

'Scary TV? No, he's not watching anything like that. Has something happened?'

'Just a moment.' Ms Haruoka stood and walked over to collect something from the staff table.

'This afternoon we had drawing time in class. Mother's Day is coming soon, and so we decided to have the children draw pictures of their mothers as presents. So . . . Well, it's about the picture Yuta drew. . . .'

Naomi gaped at the drawing Ms Haruoka handed her.

KONNO Yuta

The two people drawn on the right were clearly Yuta and Naomi. In the middle was the apartment building where they lived. He had done a good job recreating the number of floors and rooms, and he had even positioned the entrance correctly. It was much too small compared to the people, of course, but what caught her eye was the top of the picture.

The room in the centre of the top floor was covered over with a large grey scribble.

That was the room where he and Naomi lived.

'Ms Haruoka . . . Did Yuta make this grey blotch himself?'

Yuta loved drawing. When he made one he liked, he would sit and stare at it happily until bedtime. Naomi thought it adorable and privately called it his 'self-esteem time'. For Yuta to defile his own work was unimaginable. So, perhaps a child in a nearby seat had played a prank on him? She didn't want to cast suspicion on Yuta's classmates, but her mind made the leap. Haruoka had anticipated this.

'Well, there are some children who mess with others' work during drawing or craft time. They tend not to mean anything by it, but it can hurt the target's feelings. So, we teachers make it a point to keep close watch and ensure that everyone is focusing on their own work to keep things like that from happening. I can say with some confidence that today no one played any pranks with Yuta's drawing.'

'I see . . .'

'I'm sorry to say, though, that I was not able to watch closely enough to keep track of every step of every child's drawing. I didn't notice this until the drawing was finished, so I don't know exactly what was going on when Yuta made this grey smudge. I'm sorry about that.'

'There's no need to apologize. I know you have to handle a lot of children on your own. There's no way you can catch every little detail.'

'Thank you.'

'But why would he have done this?'

'Actually, I asked him earlier. And Yuta said, 'I don't want to tell.'

'He said that?'

'Yuta loves drawing so much, and usually he's happy to talk for ages about his pictures. I'm a bit worried, actually, and wondering what might be going on with him today. This building . . . It is where you live, right?'

'Yes. And the room that's scribbled out . . . That's our apartment.'

'I thought so. That's why I was wondering if anything bad had happened at home lately.'

The words sent a sharp pain through Naomi's breast as she remembered the night before.

'Ms Haruoka, actually, last night . . .'

Naomi told her about the previous night, when she had been so hard on Yuta about his scribbling on the walls. She had intended only to share the bare facts, but as she spoke, her emotions rose and before she knew it, she had confessed to all the self-recrimination she had felt.

When she finished, Ms Haruoka looked into Naomi's eyes and said, her voice full of sympathy, 'I see. But you made up after that, right?'

'We did.'

'And Yuta himself understands why you told him off, right?'

'I think . . . Yes, I am always careful to make the reasons clear, whenever I scold him.'

'If that's the case, then I don't think it can be the reason for this. Look . . .'

Ms Haruoka pointed at the mother in the drawing.

'Mama's face is drawn so prettily. If he was still upset about getting in trouble, then he wouldn't have drawn you like that.'

'Is that true?'

'Yes, so I wouldn't worry about that any more. Let's keep an eye on him for now. It might have just been a passing thing today.'

'Thank you so much. You've really set my mind at ease.'

'Oh, but I'm sorry for speaking like some kind of expert or anything! And wait a moment.' Ms Haruoka took Yuta's drawing to the office printer and made a copy.

'This is actually supposed to be a Mother's Day present, so we're keeping the drawings here until then. But I'm sure you'll be thinking about this one, so here's a copy to keep for now.'

'Thank you. That's very thoughtful of you.'

'Not at all. Oh, and let's keep it just between the two of us that I showed you Yuta's picture. It is supposed to be a surprise, after all.'

'Oh, right, of course. Hahaha, I'll practise my surprised face!'

Naomi stared intently at the copy in her hand. Then, she noticed something.

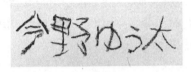

KONNO Yuta

'Did Yuta write this himself?'

'He did.'

'When did he learn to write kanji?'

'Actually, last week we all started practising writing our own names in kanji. Since the children will be going on to primary school next year, it's time they started learning.'

'Is that so!'

'I was surprised at how quickly Yuta remembered his. His first name is still a bit too difficult with all of those strokes, but now he can write his family name in kanji from memory.'

'Oh my.'

What kind of man would Yuta grow into? A kind man, but perhaps a sad one, as well.

The two went back to the classroom. Yuta had finished the puzzle and was showing it off proudly. Ms Haruoka and Naomi were both effusive in their praise, and soon Yuta was beaming bashfully. Nothing at all seemed out of the ordinary. Naomi felt a little relief.

. . .

When they left the nursery school, the sky was stained scarlet by the setting sun.

'I'm hungry,' grumbled Yuta. And so was Naomi. But she simply couldn't muster the energy to cook today.

'Hey, Yuta, why don't we eat out this evening?'

The two stopped at a casual restaurant along the way. By the time they had finished their meal and stepped outside, darkness had fallen. They set out walking, hand in hand.

They left the main thoroughfare for the neighbourhood back streets, and their building came into view. Naomi's body stiffened unconsciously in a pang of fear. She recalled the car from the day before.

It's fine . . . Right? Surely not four days in a row. . . .

Just then, like clockwork, she heard the faint hum of a car engine. The low, somehow eerie sound slowly approached. Naomi regretted not heading straight home. It was so dark out that even if something happened, no one would witness it.

'Mama, there's a car coming.'

'I know. Don't turn around.'

'Why not?'

'Because I said so, that's why.'

She could hear the sound of tires on asphalt just behind her.

Headlights shone over them both. Their shadows, one big and one small, fell on the ground before them.

'Mama.'

'Come on, Yuta, let's run.'

Naomi gripped Yuta's hand and pulled him along into a trot. When they did, the car sped up.

Why? Who is it? What do they want?

The fear and anxiety almost reduced her to tears. She wanted to be in her room, the door locked, and now. She wanted to be in a safe place.

The building entry came into view.

'Watch your feet, now, Yuta.'

They rushed up the steps, pushed the glass doors open and burst into the lobby.

The world grew bright. She had never felt so grateful for fluorescent lights before. Surely whoever it was would not follow them in here. She tried to still her trembling knees as she pushed the elevator's 'Up' button and took a deep breath. The indicator above the doors glowed '6.' It would take about ten seconds for the elevator to descend from the sixth floor.

Fearfully, she glanced towards the entrance. Something drew her attention. The glass doors were flooded with hazy light. The headlights. The car had stopped outside the building. She heard a 'clack'. The sound of a car door opening. Had the driver gotten out of the car? Surely not. . . .

The elevator passed the fourth floor. She briefly thought of fleeing to the building manager's room, but then remembered it was after hours. The manager would have gone home already. There was nowhere to run.

'Yuta, why don't we go this way?'

She pointed to the stairwell next to the elevator. Yuta did not look pleased.

'Aww . . . It's too far to the sixth floor!' And to tell the truth, Naomi had little faith that her trembling knees could manage a dash up the stairs.

She looked to the doors again. Come to think of it, it had been a while, but she hadn't heard the car door close. Perhaps the driver was just looking at them with the door open? It was a creepy thought, but it might also mean that no one would rush them.

A few seconds later, the elevator doors opened. She pulled Yuta inside and stabbed at the button for the sixth floor. The doors slowly started to close.

Faster! Faster!

And just then.

Through the shrinking gap between the doors, Naomi clearly saw someone standing outside the glass lobby doors.

He was dressed in a grey, full-length coat. His face was concealed by a hood, but she could tell from his build he was a man.

Who is he?

They reached the sixth floor. Just a few more steps to their door. The tension began to ease, and she said to Yuta as they walked down the corridor, 'Yuta, sorry I made you run like that. I bet you're all sweaty, aren't you? Jump in the bath as soon as we get home, all right?'

'I want to watch YouTube first.'

'Oh, now, you can watch once you ge—'

As she was saying that, she sensed something behind her. A presence . . . Or rather, a sound.

'Mama? What's wrong?'

71

'Sorry, Yuta. Let's hurry.'

She listened. Wheeze . . . Wheeze . . . It sounded like someone desperately trying to silence their own gasping breath. It was a low, masculine sound. Her ears told her it was coming from behind the door marked 'Stairs'. Her heart stopped in her chest.

He . . . He followed us on the stairs?

Once Naomi and Yuta had got in the elevator, had the man in the coat rushed up the stairs to head them off? But how could he have known they lived on the sixth floor? Then Naomi remembered what Yuta had said just a moment ago.

'Aww . . . It's too far to the sixth floor!'

Had he heard? From outside?

What should they do? Take the elevator back down to the ground floor and run outside? But if they did that, they'd have to go back toward the stairwell . . . No. Her whole body rebelled at the thought.

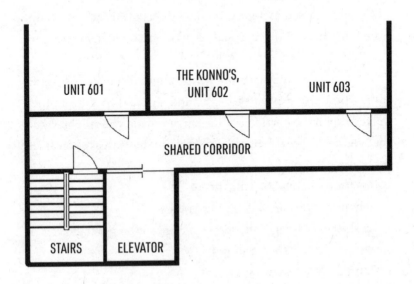

Their apartment was right there. They'd just have to get inside.

She took her key from her bag. Her hands were shaking. It took a few seconds, but she finally got the key in the lock. Just then, she heard a creak from the stairwell. It was the sound of a heavy door slowly opening.

He's coming!

Naomi focused on her fingertips to turn the key. Twisting the doorknob, the door opened. She pushed Yuta through first then slipped through the half-open door herself. She slammed it shut and, her hands trembling, set the lock and chain. She looked through the peephole. The man was not in sight. She kept looking, but he did not come.

Naomi collapsed to the floor with a gasp, all the strength escaping her.

'Mama . . . Are you okay?'

'Yeah. I'm okay. I think.'

As her reason returned, her heart began to fill with doubt. Why had the man waited? There was time between their leaving the elevator and reaching the door. He could have got to them. But he had kept waiting behind the door.

She thought about the 'creak' she had heard. Why had he opened the door just then?

'Oh no . . .'

Naomi knew she had made a terrible mistake.

The man had seen them go inside.

We showed him where we live.

That night, Naomi stayed awake until nearly dawn. She sat in the living room, constantly aware of the doorway. She kept imagining a man forcing the door open with a crowbar and storming in with a knife.

Should she call the police? But nothing had actually happened. She doubted they would see it as any sort of crime.

And above all, Naomi had her own reasons for avoiding the police.

What am I going to do? About any of it?

She moaned weakly. Then, her eyes fell on a piece of paper on the table. It was the copy of Yuta's picture she'd got from Ms Haruoka.

'I was wondering if anything bad had happened at home lately.'

Could it be that Yuta had noticed the man's presence somehow and expressed the stress of it through that picture? If that were so, then without question, things could not go on like this. She had to do something, and quickly.

Oh, Haruto . . . Please watch over us.

Naomi looked at Haruto's picture on the family altar with pleading eyes.

From four in the morning, the sky began to lighten. In a couple of hours, her usual busy day would begin again.

I have to get some sleep.

Naomi struggled to raise her leaden body and stumbled into the bedroom. She straightened Yuta's tousled bedclothes and collapsed into her futon beside his. She set her alarm for six, closed her eyes, and fell into a deep sleep in seconds.

.　　.　　.

She had a bad feeling from the moment her eyes opened. The light shining through the window was wrong. When she looked at the clock, it read half past seven.

'Oh no . . .'

She leapt up from her futon. Usually, this would be about when she left the house.

'Yuta, wake up! We overslept!'

She looked at the futon next to hers and felt a chill.

Yuta was gone.

'He must be using the toilet . . . Right?' she muttered, trying to calm herself, as she headed for the bathroom. But he was not there. Nor in the living room, or the kitchen, or on the balcony or in any of the closets. He was nowhere to be found.

Her heart was pounding in her chest.

Surely not outside? There's no way . . . Going out by himself? He'd never . . .

She slipped into her sandals and went to open the door, and then she noticed. The door was unlocked. The chain was released. She looked down . . . Yuta's shoes were gone.

Naomi's mouth gaped in a silent scream. Her voice would not come.

'Yes . . . Yes . . . Of course, all of us here will do whatever we can to help. Call us anytime. I just hope he's all right. . . . No, no. . . . It's fine, of course. . . . Yes. All right, goodbye.'

Miho Haruoka replaced the telephone handset.

'Has something happened, Ms Haruoka?' Ms Isozaki, a veteran at the nursery school, asked from beside her.

'Well . . .'

.   .   .

Just a few minutes earlier, Ms Haruoka had come to work as usual and started on her morning routine when the telephone rang. It was Naomi Konno, Yuta's mother.

'This is Naomi Konno! I'm so sorry to bother when you must be busy. Is Yuta . . . Is Yuta Konno there?'

She could tell over the phone that Naomi was in a state of panic. Ms Haruoka fell back on her Pre-K training.

'Mrs Konno? Are you all right? First, try to calm down. Breathe deeply. Inhale . . . Exhale . . . Inhale . . . Exhale . . . Can you tell me what has happened?'

Naomi remained upset but was able to explain her discovery that Yuta was gone.

'That is worrisome. . . . It doesn't look like Yuta has arrived yet.'

'I thought . . . Oh, where could he have gone?'

'Have you contacted the police?'

'The police . . .'

Naomi's voice fell, for some reason.

'No . . . I'll do that now. Uh . . . I suppose that this means he'll be taking the day off from nursery. I'll let you know as soon as I find him. I'm sorry to worry you!' Naomi said in a rush as she hung up.

· · ·

'Oh dear . . . That is a worry. Let me know if anything happens! I'd best be getting on.' Ms Isozaki listened to Ms Haruoka's story to the end, then rushed out with a few curt words. Someone else might have found her reaction a bit cold, but Ms Haruoka knew it was anything but.

Ms Isozaki was in charge of the infant class, with children under two years old. Even a few seconds of inattention could endanger a child's life. She didn't have time to spend worrying about another class's child.

Ms Haruoka sat alone in the staffroom thinking about Yuta. He had been with them for two years. Although she only watched over any child for a few years, she still ended up caring for them as if they were her own. What she really wanted was to run out and search for Yuta herself.

But soon the other children would be arriving. She had to maintain a professional demeanor, she had to focus.

Ms Haruoka stood up and headed for her classroom.

The Upper Class that Ms Haruoka headed currently had twenty-two children. With Yuta absent, there were still twenty-one others to watch. They were all over five years old, meaning they were much less trouble than Ms Isozaki's infant class. That also meant, though, that their senses of self were that much stronger, making them every bit as capable of sneakiness and guile as any adult. She couldn't simply be 'Nice Ms Haruoka'. She needed to be able to switch between the calm of the Buddha and the frightfulness of an ogre as skilfully as a Peking opera performer changing masks.

'All right, everyone, talking time is over! It's time to take the register. Answer nice and loud when I call your name.'

A few rambunctious boys pointedly ignored Ms Haruoka and kept on roughhousing.

Time for the ogre mask . . .

But just as the thought appeared in her mind, a shout cut through the boys' voices.

'Hey! Ms Haruoka! Why isn't Yuta here?'

It was Miu Yonezawa. Miu sat next to Yuta and always watched out for him. Yuta himself often seemed a bit put out by her attention, but they got along well most of the time.

'Oh, well, Yuta . . . He's off today because of some family matter.'

'What? But he didn't say anything about it yesterday! He's getting a talking to when he gets here tomorrow!'

Oh dear, Miho Haruoka thought. *I never should have made up a lie. But I can't upset the children by telling them he's gone missing.*

Naomi Konno

Talking to Ms Haruoka on the telephone had calmed Naomi down a little. And then she noticed she was still in her pajamas. She rushed to get changed, then headed for the building manager's office on the ground floor.

The fat, fifty-something manager sat typing sleepily at a computer.

'Um, excuse me. I'm Konno, in apartment 602. This morning,

it looks like my son left on his own. Is there any way you could show me the security camera footage?'

The man glanced at Naomi's face and said in an annoyed tone, 'I suppose . . . Don't get your hopes up, though. We only have the one camera on the entrance, though, what with the low building fees.'

'Of course! That should be fine.'

'Right. One moment.'

He banged away at the keyboard.

'So, about what time did your son leave?'

'I know it was before half past seven, but I can't say when exactly what time.'

'So, up to seven thirty . . . Hmm? Is this him?'

Naomi stared at the monitor through the office window. It showed Yuta running out the door on his own.

'Yes! That's him!'

Naomi pressed her hand to her chest.

Yuta was on his own. So, that meant the man from the night before wasn't involved.

'I'm sorry to have bothered you when you're so busy. Thank you,' she said.

'No, not at all, I'm hardly busy. But he's still so little, you must be really worried. Would you like me to call the police?"

'No, that's fine.'

Miho Haruoka

Morning at the nursery school sped along at its usual pace.

After lunch was over, it was nap time for the children. The minders who were not on nap duty all went back to the staffroom.

79

It was a short respite when they could do their administrative work without distraction.

Ms Haruoka sat at her desk and started her paperwork. But she struggled to concentrate. She couldn't stop thinking about Yuta. She'd been able to distract herself all morning while caring for the children. There hadn't been any word from Naomi since that one telephone call. She must not have found him yet.

Ms Haruoka suddenly recalled the picture from the other day.

She took Yuta's drawing out of the file and stared at it. The apartment that had been scribbled out with grey. This picture, and the morning's disappearance. Could they be connected?

He scribbled out his own home. What could be the psychology behind that?

Ms Haruoka thought back to her time studying to become a Pre-K teacher.

A special lecturer had once come for a guest lecture in her developmental psychology class. The topic had been 'pictures'. The older woman stressed the importance of pictures in understanding the minds of children.

.　　.　　.

'Whenever I tell this story, people always seem so surprised,' the professor said as she drew a diamond shape on the chalkboard. 'This is a rhombus. You could also call it a diamond. Now, everyone, please try drawing this shape in your notebooks.'

The young Miho Haruoka wondered briefly why they were being asked to do such a pointless exercise, but she obliged, drawing a diamond on a sheet of loose-leaf paper.

'Did you all do it? Did anyone find it too difficult?' the professor asked facetiously. A few giggles ran through the classroom.

'No one? Of course not. An adult should have no trouble. However, what if we asked a small child to try?'

The lecturer stuck a sheet of paper to the board.

'This is a diamond drawn by my nephew, Kensuke. He drew it when he was three.'

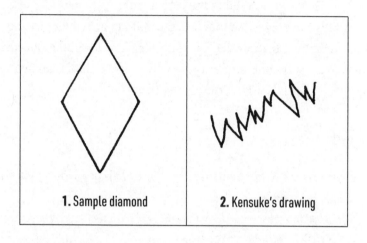

| 1. Sample diamond | 2. Kensuke's drawing |

The room filled with muttering. The picture was simply a jagged line.

'Do any of you think this looks like a rhombus? Of course not. Kensuke drew this from a reference picture and tried his best to make it look identical. And the result is this jagged line. He wasn't playing some kind of prank. And he wasn't suffering from any developmental problems. The fact is that many children draw a diamond the same way.'

The professor's words caught her students' attention, which seemed to please her. She continued, now sporting a smug look on her face.

'When Kensuke looked at the reference picture, this is what occurred to him: "If I touched it, it would hurt." Look, the diamond's points do look sharp, don't they? So, in his mind, he imagined what it would feel like if he touched those points. Children have powerful imaginations, and the possibility of pain consumed him. He expressed the pain of that pointiness in his picture.'

The professor pointed at the jagged line.

'Adults can draw what they see, the real thing, in their pictures. Children, though, draw the "idea" of what appears in their heads. Like an artist. People sometimes say that every child is an artist, and I feel that is not far from the truth.'

.   .   .

The professor's words echoed in Ms Haruoka's head as she stared at Yuta's picture.

Children don't draw the thing that they see with their eyes, they draw the idea in their minds. . . . So, when Yuta drew this picture, an image of a 'grey mess' is what he had in his head.

Ms Haruoka wanted to know what Yuta had felt. She took the picture back to the classroom.

Sitting in the empty classroom, Ms Haruoka took crayons and paper from the staff desk. She looked at the picture as she copied it. It probably wouldn't tell her anything, but the act itself might help her get into the same headspace as Yuta.

She picked up the black crayon. *First, he would have drawn the shape of the building on the paper.* She drew as she imagined he had done. Then, with the grey crayon, she scribbled out the centre of the sixth floor.

When she did, the black crayon outlining the building mixed with the grey, leaving an unpleasant colour. It felt somehow off. *This is wrong.*

She compared her picture and Yuta's and noticed a small difference.

Ms Haruoka's drawing

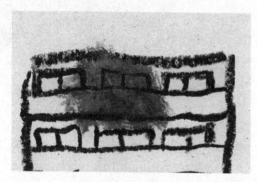

Yuta's drawing

The black and grey crayon weren't smudged in Yuta's picture.

The section that had been scribbled out in grey still had clean black lines. The grey scribbles were so forceful that any lines underneath should certainly have been smudged and smeared. Why were the lines so clean?

Ms Haruoka sat deep in thought for a time, then suddenly arrived at a very simple conclusion.

'Of course. He must have drawn the building afterwards.'

Yuta hadn't scribbled out any part of the apartment building in grey. First, he had scribbled out a section of the paper, and then drawn the building over it. The black lines went over the grey. That explained the lack of smearing. But then . . .

'Why did he do it at all?'

She looked once more at the picture. Then, her eyes fell on one detail.

The very edge of the grey scribble overlapped the line marking the building's border. That was the only part where the black line smeared with the grey.

Meaning, the border lines were the only part drawn before the grey scribble. Ms Haruoka tried to rearrange her disordered mind.

First, Yuta had drawn the large rectangle that made up the building's shape. Then, he had coloured the upper part in grey and drawn the apartments over it. Shape → grey → apartment. What did this strange order mean?

The staffroom door suddenly opened. Ms Haruoka looked up and saw Ms Isozaki standing there.

'Sorry to burst in on you! Have they found Yuta yet?' she asked.

'No, I don't think so.'

'I see. So, why do you suppose the police haven't come?'

'Pardon?'

'You know, at the nursery school where I worked before, we had a similar incident. It was a six-year-old girl that time. Anyway, one day she disappeared from home, and the police went into quite a frenzy. They found her right away, though. She'd gone off to see her grandmother who lived in the next town over. Of course, everyone was just happy she was safe. But that morning, a patrolman came to the nursery and asked all kinds of questions. It was quite a nuisance, actually. I'm just wondering why no one's come this time.'

'Now that you mention it, it is odd.'

'I suppose the police just have a different strategy this time. I am sorry for interrupting when you must be busy.'

'No, not at all. Thank you for being so concerned.'

'What is it you're working on there, anyway?'

'Oh, this . . .'

Ms Haruoka told Ms Isozaki what she'd been thinking about.

'I was just wondering what Yuta was feeling when he scribbled this part out. What do you think, Ms Isozaki?'

'I see . . . I think he might have been correcting something.'

'Correcting? How?'

'Well, you can't erase crayons like a pencil, right? So, that's why you see lots of children scribble things out when they make mistakes on a drawing.'

85

'Right . . .'

'Oh, sorry! I have to go! Let me know if you find out anything!'

Ms Isozaki ran off down the corridor.

Ms Haruoka, left alone in the staffroom, sat in silence.

Why hadn't she thought of that before? Perhaps she had been too caught up in the bizarre idea of Yuta scribbling out his own home.

Scribbling out a mistake . . . That was a real possibility.

Her eyes fell on her crayon box. What colour did children use when they tried to erase a drawing mistake? She didn't even have to think about it. White.

That was something her adult sensibilities could grasp. Just like she would use white-out to cover up a mistake in pen on a document, a child would use white to scribble out a drawing mistake. But, unlike white-out, scribbling over something in crayon would mix the colours.

Meaning, Yuta had not used a grey crayon. He had tried to erase a drawing done in black crayon using white. The result was that the two colours had mixed and made this grey blotch.

Ms Haruoka hurried to the children's lockers at the back of the room. She opened Yuta's and took out his box of crayons. She opened it and checked his white crayon. The tip was blunted and smeared with grey. She had been right. It had got discoloured when he scribbled out the black picture.

Ms Haruoka thought back over what she knew.

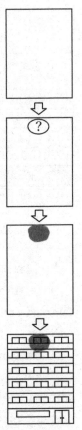

'First, Yuta drew the outline of the building. Then, he drew something with a black crayon. Then, deciding that was a mistake, he had scribbled it out with white. The white and black smeared together to make grey. Then he drew the apartments over that and finished the building.'

So then, what had he scribbled out? If she learned that, she could find the truth of this picture.

'If only I'd been watching him more attentively . . .'

But as she voiced this, it dawned on her. . . . Someone had been.

There is someone in this nursery school who does watch Yuta closely, all the time. Ms Haruoka headed to the nap room to find her.

·   ·   ·

There were still about twenty minutes left in naptime, but several of the children were already awake, fidgeting in their futons. Miu Yonezawa was one of them.

Ms Haruoka got permission from the naptime minder, then led Miu to the next room.

'I'm sorry to disrupt your naptime, Miu.'

'It's okay. I'm not tired any more, anyway.'

'Thank you. Listen, do you remember when everyone drew a picture yesterday?'

'Yeah! I drew my mummy.'

'That's right! Well, I'm trying to remember what kind of picture Yuta drew, but I can't remember at all.'

'What? You forgot already?'

'I did. Do you remember?'

'Yeah! Um, he drew a building, and Yuta and his mummy were standing there.'

'You've got a good memory, Miu!'

'Hee-hee!'

'So then, I'm wondering how Yuta drew that picture. Miu, did you watch how he did it?'

'Yeah! I did!'

Ms Haruoka's pulse quickened.

'Can you tell me how he did it?'

'Sure! Um, let's see, first, Yuta drew a big rectangle with his crayon.'

'A big rectangle? Hmm. And what then?'

'Then, a little triangle.'

'A triangle?'

'Yeah! A little triangle inside the big rectangle. Then, after that . . . Um . . .'

But from that point on, Miu admitted she had been so intent on her own picture that she couldn't recall what Yuta had done.

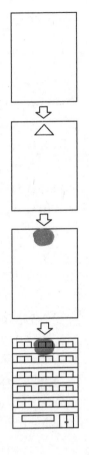

·   ·   ·

Ms Haruoka thanked Miu and took her back to the nap room, then returned to her own classroom. She had learned something valuable from Miu.

'Yuta first drew a rectangle, then a small triangle inside it. He scribbled that out with white, then drew the apartments over it and completed his picture of the building.'

His actions told her one thing.

Yuta had at first wanted to draw something other than an apartment building.

A drawing with a small triangle inside a large rectangle . . .
If he had continued, he would have had a completely different
picture.

But along the way, he decided to draw something else. Sitting
in front of his incomplete drawing, he must have suddenly
thought:

If I draw rooms on this, it will look like an apartment building.

It was like writing the wrong letter, then writing over it to try
to make it look like the right one. So, why had Yuta done that?

In Ms Haruoka's class, she had a policy of handing out new
paper whenever anyone made a mistake. Yuta himself had come
asking for refills plenty of times before. So then, why did he
redraw his picture yesterday? There was only one reason she
could think of.

He wanted to hide it. Whatever his original drawing was going
to be, he decided to hide it.

He didn't want Ms Haruoka to know he had tried to draw
something else.

What could he have been drawing that he didn't want Ms
Haruoka to know about? Ms Haruoka decided to rethink from
the bottom up.

The original assignment had
been for the children to draw pictures of their mothers. And in Yuta's
picture, he and his mother had been
standing there, hand in hand. Now
another doubt began to form in Ms
Haruoka's mind.

Which had Yuta drawn first, the
people, or the shape?

She thought back on her conversation with Miu, who had said:
Um, let's see, first, Yuta drew a big rectangle with his crayon.
Meaning, he had drawn the shape first. That confused her.

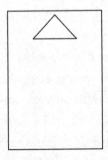

When asked to draw a picture of 'mother', the first thing Yuta had drawn was a shape. Why was that? Thinking about it, Ms Haruoka had an unfathomable thought.

Could that shape have actually been a picture of Yuta's mother?

At first glance, it was a lifeless object, certainly not anything that resembled Naomi. However . . .

'*Adults can draw what they see, the real thing, in their pictures. Children, though, draw the "idea" of what appears in their heads.*'

When Yuta started to draw a picture of his mother, he had—perhaps unconsciously—started drawing this shape. That was the idea that appeared in his mind when he thought of the word 'mother'. But, for Yuta, it was something forbidden, something to hide.

The realization triggered something in her brain that made all the scattered pieces of information fall into place. Like a jigsaw puzzle, it created a picture . . . A terrible one.

.   .   .

Naomi Konno must have abused Yuta.

She didn't want to believe it. She wanted it to be a mistake.

Ms Haruoka rearranged the pieces in her mind as she walked down the corridor to the staffroom. But no matter how many times she did, the picture did not change. She couldn't think of any other way to make everything come together.

Why hadn't the police been in touch?

Because Naomi had never contacted them. She wanted nothing to do with the police because of some past offense.

Why had Yuta suddenly left the house without a word?

Because he wanted to escape from Naomi, didn't he?

And above all, there was his drawing. The shapes had reminded Ms Haruoka of something.

A rectangle with a triangular hole. Like you would see in a stencil ruler.

Just two days ago, Yuta had used his ruler to scribble on the walls, and Naomi had scolded him for it. And then, yesterday afternoon, she had asked the children to draw a picture of their mother. Yuta had tried to imagine Naomi's smile, her kind voice, her comforting smell . . . But what had actually appeared in his mind was the stencil ruler.

The memory of that scolding must have settled into Yuta like a deep trauma.

But could a simple telling-off truly cause such emotional distress?

At that thought, the image of Naomi from the day before rose unbidden in Ms Haruoka's mind.

Her weeping face, filled with guilt . . . You might almost have thought she was paying penance for something. Ms Haruoka had never seen a parent so filled with regret over disciplining their child. If the parents of small children cried

91

every time they had to be strict, they'd weep themselves dry on a daily basis.

Clearly, she had gone beyond a simple scolding.

And yet, it was hard to believe that the doting Naomi would ever be capable of actually punching or kicking Yuta. Perhaps it fell more along the lines of a strong spanking. That first hint of violence from his mama, whom he had trusted so deeply, could well have gnawed at Yuta, and caused him to associate pain with the image of the ruler.

But even if her theory was correct, Ms Haruoka had no desire to accuse Naomi of anything. Holding down a job and being a single mother was no mean feat. Every day was likely a struggle. Exhaustion, worry, loneliness . . . They had all piled up and culminated in a raised hand. It could happen to anyone.

But the problem was, Naomi wouldn't contact the police because she was afraid it would come out, and in the meantime, Yuta was in danger. He could have an accident or be abducted. Ms Haruoka wanted to talk to Naomi, to tell her that it would be all right. That no one would blame her. She should talk to the police and find Yuta as quickly as possible.

As soon as she got to the staffroom, Ms Haruoka dialled Naomi's number.

Naomi Konno

'Never call this number again! I never want to hear your voice as long as I live!'

Naomi screamed into her phone, forgetting where she was, standing on a quiet residential street. It felt like all the strength in her body focused through her finger as she stabbed the 'End

92

Call' button. She wanted to throw her phone to the ground and shatter it.

Naomi had been combing the neighbourhood since morning looking for Yuta. She had gone door to door asking after him. And then had come the call from Yuta's nursery, from his teacher Ms Haruoka.

And Ms Haruoka had said things Naomi could never forgive.

That piece of garbage! Accusing me of abusing Yuta?

It was unbearable. To think, someone she had trusted now considered her a child abuser!

I could never! It's unthinkable! I have never raised my hand to Yuta, not once since the day he was born!

When I was little, of course, it was normal for parents to hit their children. My own mother did it. And that's exactly why, when I became a mother, I swore I would never do the same.

I'm not a perfect parent, I know that. But I would never hurt Yuta. I am certain of that. I swear to God!

In her head, the words were a scream.

Unnoticed, tears spilled from her eyes. She felt as if her very existence had been denied.

But, ironically, thanks to Ms Haruoka, she now knew where Yuta had gone.

A triangle inside a rectangle. That wasn't a stencil ruler. It must have been . . .

She opened the contacts app on her phone. She scrolled down and down, searching for a number she hadn't used in years. For the place Yuta must be right now.

She heard the ringing on the other end, and then a man answered, his voice tired.

'Thank you for calling. This is Sakura Memorial Garden.'

93

'I'm sorry to bother you, but I have a question. Is there perhaps a young boy visiting right now?'

'Oh! Are you looking for Yuta, by any chance?'

'Yes! That's right!'

'Oh, thank goodness! Please, don't worry. He's here with me right now.'

As the morning's tension finally flooded from her body, Naomi lost the strength to stand. She slumped to her knees on the spot.

'Th-thank you. I'll be right over.'

.   .   .

Sakura Memorial Garden was a cemetery some ten minutes' walk from Naomi's building. Despite its close proximity, Naomi had not visited in years. Indeed, she had gone to the trouble of avoiding even passing through its neighbourhood. It did not bring happy memories.

She stepped into the small office near the park entrance and spoke to the older man sitting at the reception desk.

'Excuse me. I'm Naomi Konno. We spoke on the phone?'

The man smiled widely when he saw Naomi.

'Hello! We've been expecting you.'

'I am so sorry for all of the trouble.'

'Not at all! It was nothing. Yuta's waiting in the back. Come right this way.'

As they walked, the man told her what had happened.

'I guess it was about an hour ago. A couple who had come to visit their family grave stopped by the office and told me that there was a little boy wandering around the cemetery. They were worried he'd got lost. So, I went to check it out. He was wandering around like he was looking for something. I was worried, so I asked what the matter was. He said, "I'm looking for my mother's grave." Well, that certainly touched me. As small as he is and all, coming alone to visit his mother . . . What a fine boy.'

I knew it . . . Naomi thought. Yuta had come to see his birth mother.

That rectangle with a triangle in it . . . Yuta had been trying to draw a gravestone. He had been writing the first character of their name, Konno 今, but had stopped. Miu Yonezawa had seen the top of the character and mistaken it for a triangle.

And that meant that Yuta . . .

Yuta Konno

The only sound left in his memories was the thunderous chorus of cicadas.

Yuta stood under the brilliant blue sky in his straw hat. His father Haruto was saying something in his kind voice. But Yuta could not remember his words.

But he remembered that they were standing in front of a big rock. It was a rectangle. And there were six symbols carved into it.

He didn't learn the word 'gravestone' until much later. When he was four, his teacher at nursery was reading a picture book, and a picture of one came up.

A rectangular stone. Yuta knew as soon as he saw it. That day, he and his father had seen a grave. And the teacher had told them, 'A person who has passed away is sleeping under this stone.'

Yuta had thought, *Who was sleeping under that rock we saw?*

And then, just the other day, Yuta finally figured it out. Ms Haruoka had said, 'Everyone, remember you all joined the upper class from April. Now, you're the oldest boys and girls here! And I think you all know, that means next year you'll move on to primary school. There is so much more fun stuff at school. Even more than here. And you'll make new friends, too! But that also means you'll have a lot more to do.

'For example, right now everyone writes their name in hiragana, right? Well, when you get to school, you'll have to use kanji to do it. So, today, we're all going to practise writing our names in kanji to prepare for next year! I'm going to give everyone a piece of paper. It has your name written in kanji on it. When you get it, try tracing it with your finger!'

The piece of paper she gave to Yuta had the kanji 今野優太 (KONNO Yuta) written on it. It was the first time he had seen his own name in kanji before . . . Or, it should have been.

今野 . . . He felt like he knew those symbols.

Then, as if from far away, a memory seemed to rise in his brain.

The painfully loud buzz of cicadas. The bright sunlight.

His father is standing next to him. He is pointing at a gravestone. There are six symbols carved in it. They are kanji. And the first two are 今野. Konno. His name.

He could hear his father's voice now, his quiet, kind voice.

'This is where your mummy is resting. She died when you were born, Yuta.'

'What? But Mama is alive.'

'That's right. That's your mama, but you also had a mummy.'

Mama and mummy . . . Yuta started to understand, if vaguely, that he somehow had two mothers.

Mama is the kind, fun and sometimes scary woman that takes care of me, the mama that I love more than anyone in the world. He knew that Mama was also named Naomi.

And here is Mummy. . . . But who is she? He didn't know her face, or her name. But he did know that she must be a very important person for him, and for his father.

His father patted him on his hatted head and said:

'But listen, Yuta. Don't talk about Mummy in front of your mama, all right? Can you promise me that?'

'. . . Okay.'

'Thank you. If you want to know about your mummy, then ask me any time. I'll tell you everything. I promise.'

But he had died before he could keep that promise.

And that is why the only memory Yuta had of his mummy was that day. And even that memory eventually got buried somewhere deep in his mind. Maybe because of his worry about Mama.

But then, after years, Yuta remembered.

That he had a mummy. And that she was resting in her grave.

.   .   .

It was a few days after they first learned kanji.

During drawing time, Ms Haruoka said, 'Mother's Day is coming up. So, let's draw a picture as a present for Mummy!'

Yuta didn't feel very excited about it. The night before, he had got in trouble over a drawing he did, and he and Mama were still at odds.

When he picked up his crayon, something bubbled up in his chest.

It was a cheeky feeling. He thought he would try drawing his mummy, instead of Mama. To get back at her for scolding him.

Yuta started drawing the gravestone. That was the only memory he had of Mummy, after all. But . . . He stopped before he was through. He started to feel it was too far.

After some deep thought, he figured out how to redraw his picture to hide it.

But even then, he couldn't stop thinking about his mummy.

That night, he lay in his futon thinking.

I want to see Mummy. I want to go back one more time.

The next morning, Yuta set out alone for the very first time in his life.

He didn't really remember the way to the grave. He just walked the path that he foggily recalled taking with his father.

The fact that he made it without getting lost, without asking anyone for help, and in only a few dozen minutes, could almost be called a miracle. Yuta didn't know that word, but he did feel that something had guided him.

When he arrived, the gate to the cemetery was closed. He decided to wait at a nearby park until it opened. He was aware that he was doing something wrong, so he hid inside the playground tunnel so no one would see him.

He spent the longest, most anxious hours of his life. And then ten came around. When he saw that the gate was open, he ran through at full speed. Holding his pounding chest, he searched for the grave.

But the cemetery was larger than he had thought, and the layout more complicated, so he struggled to find it. He walked in circles for a long time. His feet were tired. He was hungry. He was thirsty. And he wanted to go home. But when he got home, Mama would be angry. He was filled with despair.

And then, an old man came walking up.

'Hey there, what's wrong? Did you lose your mum or dad?'

The man led him away, and Yuta followed him into the building near the cemetery's entrance. The man asked his name and gave him some cold barley tea and rice crackers. It was his first meal of the day. He devoured it like he was starving.

'Yuta! Your mama called. Isn't that great? She's coming to pick you up right now,' the man said. He had a smile on his face, but Yuta's heart sank.

Mama was coming. He was going to be in so much trouble. He was afraid. He wanted to run away.

Yuta's mama had never hit him. But he was ready for it this time. He knew that what he had done was that bad.

Which was why, when Mama came into the room and simply took him in her arms, without saying a word, shock won out over happiness.

'Yuta! Oh, thank goodness. Thank goodness. You're alive. Thank goodness . . .'

When he heard Mama crying, Yuta noticed that he had started crying, too.

Naomi Konno

She had planned to give him a real tongue lashing.

'How could you worry me like that?' 'What if you'd got in an accident?!' 'What if someone had taken you?!'

But all the words she'd rehearsed simply disappeared at the sight of Yuta's face.

All she could do was squeeze him close.

Yuta was alive. She felt that was joy enough.

'Oh, it is such a lucky thing you could find him before he had an accident.'

Naomi came to herself at the sound of the man's voice.

'I truly am sorry for all the trouble.'

'It was nothing at all! Oh! Sorry to change the subject, but what was Yuta's mother's name again?'

'Her name?'

'Right. I just checked, and there are three graves with the family name of Konno. I couldn't take Yuta to his mother's without knowing her full name.'

'Yuta's mother was . . . Yuki. Yuki Konno.'

.   .   .

The man led Naomi and Yuta to the grave.

HERE LIES YUKI KONNO

It had been five years since she had last seen that inscription, at the Buddhist rite commemorating the first anniversary of Yuki's death.

It did not read 'The Grave of the Konno Family' because she had wanted it to be for Yuki alone. She never wanted to have anything to do with that woman again. That is how much Naomi feared Yuki. Naomi felt like there was a curse surrounding the woman.

When Haruto died, Naomi had taken his body to a cemetery a full hour away by train. Such was her fear that Haruto's and Yuki's spirits might be joined again after death. Even now, she wanted to grab Yuta's hand and drag him away.

But when she saw his face, gazing up at the grave with a contemplative look, she couldn't do it. No matter how much it hurt, the fact remained that Yuki was Yuta's true mother.

Naomi whispered to Yuta, 'Yuta, put your hands together. That's right. Now, close your eyes, and speak to her in your heart.'

.   .   .

It was after two when the pair left Sakura Memorial Garden.

'Now, Yuta, we're going to your nursery. We both have to apologize to your teacher for worrying her.'

'. . . Okay.'

And Naomi had something else to apologize for. She had let her feelings get the best of her and blown up at Ms Haruoka, but, reflecting on it now, the teacher was really only concerned for Yuta's welfare.

And she would be looking after him in the future. She couldn't let things stand as they were.

The two walked along, hand in hand.

Miho Haruoka

'I deeply apologize for all of the trouble we've caused,' Naomi said as she bowed over and over, standing there in the staffroom.

Ms Haruoka reassured Naomi that she, too, had felt miserable since their earlier phone call.

'No, I should never have leapt to such conclusions. Please, accept my apologies.'

'Oh, please don't. If I had been fulfilling my responsibilities . . . Come, now, Yuta, apologize to Ms Haruoka.'

'I'm sorry, Ms Haruoka.' Yuta gave a little bow of his head.

'It's all right, Yuta. But you know you shouldn't go out on your own without Mama's permission.'

She had intended to be firm with him but couldn't keep her voice from trembling.

.   .   .

Naomi and Yuta both looked exhausted, so they went straight home.

Ms Haruoka saw them off at the gate.

'See you tomorrow, then, Yuta. Bye-bye!'

'Bye-bye, Ms Haruoka!'

Ms Haruoka watched them walk off, hand in hand, with a light heart. Those two, at least, were so close that abuse was simply out of the question.

'I still have a lot to learn . . .' she muttered to herself.

On the way back to her classroom, Ms Isozaki called out to her in the corridor:

'Ms Haruoka! I heard they found Yuta. Thank goodness!'

'They did! Sorry for all the worry today.'

'Not at all. And I'm sorry for not doing a single thing to help! So, have they already left? Yuta and his grandmother?'

Ms Haruoka froze for an instant, speechless.

At that moment, Miu came racing out of the classroom. She must have been eavesdropping, because she immediately corrected Ms Isozaki:

'Ms Isozaki! That's wrong! Not "grandmother"; she's Yuta's mama!'

'Mama? But . . .'

Ms Isozaki seemed puzzled, and Miho Haruoka wanted to explain, but struggled to find a way to convey the complexities of the Konno household.

Seeing Ms Haruoka's trouble, Miu shook her head in exasperation and offered a helping hand. The words she used were quite grown-up and made one wonder where she'd learned them, but they summed things up nicely.

'Listen, Ms Isozaki. We've all got our skeletons in the closet.'

Naomi Konno

That evening, Naomi stood in front of the bathroom mirror and noticed she'd gone the whole day without make-up. She'd been so intent on hunting for Yuta from the moment she woke up that she'd totally forgotten to put on her face.

As understandable as it was, she couldn't help but feel some shock at the thought of all those people seeing her like this. Naomi was aware that she looked much older than other women her age. Like an old woman. Far older than her sixty-four years.

.   .   .

Naomi peeked into the bedroom to find Yuta sound asleep. He must have been so tired. Naomi certainly was. She went back to the living room and sat on the sofa. It had been a long day.

She glanced over at the Buddhist altar. Looking at the picture of her smiling son standing there, she whispered:

'Haruto . . . We went to that woman's grave today.'

Yuki . . . A name she never wanted to hear again.

Haruto's wife. Naomi's daughter-in-law.

She took out her phone and opened a web browser. She looked at the blog that Haruto had kept before his death.

It's dangerous to post personal information on the web.

Haruto had listened to Naomi and used a pseudonym instead of his real name.

He'd used 'Raku'. When she asked why, he'd suddenly grown bashful.

'There's a little trick to it. I took my name and—'

Ding!

As if to wake Naomi from her reverie, the doorbell rang.

She glanced at the clock. It was after ten. Who would be coming at such an hour?

A chill ran down her spine.

She tiptoed over to the door and glanced through the peephole.

The man in the grey coat stood outside.

And finally . . . He'd come to their home.

She did not know who he was, or why he was after them.

But if she did nothing, Yuta could be in danger. She had to put a stop to it before anything happened. Naomi snuck away from the door and quietly locked the bedroom door. Then she headed to the kitchen, took up a knife, and hid it behind her body.

'Yes, I'm coming!' She put on a cheerful voice and walked loudly towards the hall. She unchained and unlocked the door.

She thought back on the manager's words: *Don't get your hopes up, though. We only have the one camera on the entrance, though, what with the low building fees.*

There was no camera in the corridor.

She slowly opened the door.

The man standing there was not large, but he had an oddly

intimidating aura. Naomi almost faltered. But she did not let it overpower her. She forced a smile and beckoned:

'Please, come in!'

The man did as she said and stepped inside.

She closed the door. Now, no one could see what was going to happen.

Naomi brought the knife from behind her back and pointed it at him.

He did not move, just stood staring silently at the blade. Naomi felt another chill.

She did not know what he was after. What would he do next?

But now was her only chance.

It took no time for her to decide. She gripped the knife in both hands and thrust it into the man.

.   .   .

She had expected a fight.

But to her surprise, the man had not resisted. He fell to the floor, one hand pressed to his belly to staunch the flow of blood from the stab wound.

His hood fell away, revealing his face.

It was the wrinkled face of an old man.

Naomi seemed to recognize it from somewhere.

But she could not remember where.

CHAPTER THREE

The Art Teacher's Final Drawing

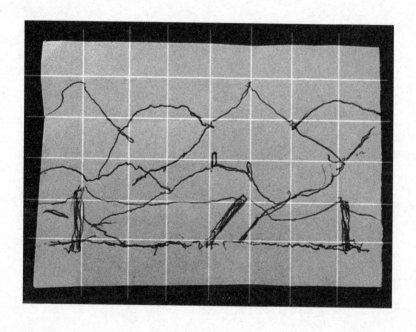

Yoshiharu Miura

From the moment he became a teacher, Yoshiharu Miura hardly spared a moment for himself. His weekdays were devoted to classes, and after school he was busy counselling students or leading clubs. Then, when finished, he was occupied with administrative work until late in the evening.

On his days off, he would sacrifice sleep to take his family out to a park where they pitched tents, fired up the grill and cooked a load of meat.

And that wasn't all.

He would talk to his friends for hours when they had problems, help find them work and sometimes bailed them out when they had financial trouble.

Students, family, friends . . . Their happiness was Miura's sole reason for living. And he never asked for anything in return.

But even Miura took a day for himself a few times a year.

He would hike up a mountainside near his house and draw the scenery he saw from the top. For him, those days represented the peak of luxury.

And today was just one of those days.

But now, what spread out before him was a vision of hell.

It was a scene of despair; a sight that turned his entire life into a lie.

Miura teased a pen from his pocket.

He had to draw.

To keep them safe.

.   .   .

On September 21, 1992, the body of a man was discovered on the side of Mt K— in L— Prefecture. The deceased was forty-one-year-old Yoshiharu Miura, who lived nearby. He was a high school art teacher.

The body had suffered numerous stab wounds and showed other signs of violence, so the case was being handled as a murder. A police investigation showed that Miura had come to Mt K— for an overnight camping trip on the 20th.

At the scene, **they discovered a drawing presumably left by Miura.**

Statement 1: Person who found the body

'My job is general upkeep for the amenities on the mountain. On the morning of the twenty-first I hiked up to check for damage on the mountain trail. Then I saw someone on the ground . . . I'm sorry. I feel sick just thinking about it. Anyway, he was in a terrible state. . . . Yes, I came down the mountain immediately and contacted the police. . . . The deceased was a schoolteacher, right? He was so young, and I understand he had a wife and child at home. . . . It's just so sad.'

110

Statement 2: Student of Yoshiharu Miura

'That's right. I'm head of the art club. Mr Miura was our club adviser, so we were in close contact. . . . What about him? If I'm honest, I didn't much care for him. Actually, I quite disliked him. . . . No, I'm not the only one. Hardly any of the students at school actually liked Mr Miura. He was so quick to anger. . . . He probably thought of himself as some kind of passionate educator or whatever, but honestly we all thought he was a pain. He yelled at me all the time when he was giving me guidance for the club. . . . It really scared me. . . . His death is a shock, but honestly, I'm not sad about it at all.'

Statement 3: Yoshiharu Miura's wife

'You want to know about . . . my husband's death? It doesn't feel real to me yet. Let me be frank with you. We were not a particularly close couple. We fought over parenting styles. . . . Well, for example, our son likes to stay in and read, but my husband kept dragging him out and making him go camping or have cookouts. . . . Our son hated it. He would just do what he wanted, with no regard for our son, and he was so self-satisfied. All "I'm a good dad, devoted to my family." . . . Forgive me. I suppose it sounds like I'm speaking ill of the dead. . . . I'm sure as time passes I'll start to feel the sadness. There were things I didn't like, but he was my one and only husband.'

Statement 4: Friend of Yoshiharu Miura

'Yoshiharu and I have been friends since our art school days. He looked out for me after we graduated, too. I have a weekly gig as a special lecturer for the art club at the school where he worked. . . . Of course, he got me the job. I guess he was worried about me

111

working some minimum-wage part-time thing. He said I should get a second job to help pay the bills. I mean, I'm grateful, of course. I was grateful but . . . Well. If you ask how much I liked the guy . . . it's not so simple. He tended to do just what he wanted and expected me to go along. He'd call me up and say, "Let's go hiking tomorrow!" or "Let's go for a drink!" without even considering I might have other plans. . . . I mean, I could have refused, but what with all he's done for me, it was a bit hard to say, "I don't want to" . . .'

(Interviews by Isamu Kumai for *L— Daily*)

.   .   .

August 28, 1995, Head Office of L— Daily, *regional newspaper for L— Prefecture*

Shunsuke Iwata, nineteen years old, sat staring at the thick folder and gulped.

The cover read 'Mt K— art teacher murder (1992), investigation materials'. It was packed with data on a gruesome murder that had occurred three years earlier.

His boss, Kumai, stood next to him. He said, 'Iwata, you sure you're ready?'

'. . . Yeah.'

'All right, then. Let's open it up.'

Kumai flipped the folder open.

Shunsuke Iwata

Shunsuke Iwata had just joined *L— Daily* that year. Three years before, a certain event had inspired him to become a newspaper reporter, and he'd come knocking on the door of the local paper as soon as he left school.

In his interview, he had been emphatic: 'I want to see the truth with my own eyes and share what I learn with people.' The interviewer had seemed satisfied, and he received a job offer immediately.

Iwata had been elated, thinking, 'I'm a reporter now!' but his hopes were dashed as soon as he started at the company.

Iwata's first posting was in the administrative department, nothing at all to do with reporting.

Iwata learned the truth only later.

L— *Daily* was a company with more than three hundred employees, and fewer than half were reporters. They were all stars working in the editorial department, the company's elite, and all were college graduates.

Iwata hadn't got the job because of his journalistic zeal. He had been one of the few non-college-educated applicants that year, who could be hired for less than what a graduate would demand.

Of course, Iwata knew that the admin workers supporting those reporters behind the scenes were important, but he was still dissatisfied. His only reason for applying at a newspaper had been the hope of becoming a reporter.

Isamu Kumai

The company had left twenty-three-year veteran Isamu Kumai in charge of Iwata's training. Kumai had once been in the editorial department and had written plenty of articles as a reporter.

At the time, his nickname had been 'Kumai the Fixer'. No one could beat him when it came to getting inside scoops on ongoing

113

criminal investigations. Not that he was especially talented. He had just thrown himself into the work, without any care for himself.

Day or night, he would race to the scene as soon as he caught wind of a crime. He would track down and interview everyone involved, and kept walking his beat in the heavy rain or blazing sun. He developed close relationships with detectives, sometimes getting down on his knees to beg for information that otherwise wouldn't be made public.

He ran flat out, all the time. And he was proud of it.

And then, three years ago, he had finally tripped and fallen.

While Kumai was in the middle of an important story, he was diagnosed with oesophageal cancer and had to take extended leave. It frustrated him deeply. It was the first time he had ever had to give up on a story in his career. The case had been the 'Mt K— art teacher murder'.

He had thrown himself into treatment with the idea that, as soon as he recovered, he'd get right back to reporting. His cooperation and care paid off, and two months later he was cleared to go back to work.

But that first day, the head of the paper called him and dealt another blow.

'Kumai, you've done well for us. But you know as well as I that reporters whittle away their lives for a pay cheque. With you being sick already, it'd be too much to ask. So, get down to the administrative department. From now on, you take care of yourself with a lighter workload.'

He had been reassigned. Now that Kumai was ill and couldn't afford to push himself so hard, he no longer had any value as a reporter. Or that's what he'd been told.

114

Kumai resisted. He insisted over and over that they at least let him finish his reporting on the Mt K— case, but they didn't budge.

.   .   .

Three years had passed.

In the spring of 1995, a new hire joined the administrative section. He was a kid, just out of high school, name of Shunsuke Iwata. He said he'd joined the company hoping to become a reporter, but he'd been put in administration against his wishes. Which was not that uncommon. Employees' lives and careers both depended on the company's whims. Even knowing that, Kumai couldn't help but feel sorry for the kid.

It was partly because his predicament reflected Kumai's own . . . Wanting to be a reporter but being thwarted from becoming one.

Still, Kumai had a job to do, and it wouldn't do to pamper him, so he hardened his heart and trained the kid without relent. Iwata himself, as if rising to the challenge, learned well and quickly. Eventually, not even six months after joining, he had grown into a vital asset for the administrative team.

One day, not long after, Iwata came to Kumai at the end of the work day. He wore a brooding expression on his face. 'Mr Kumai,' he said, 'I'd like to ask your advice about something.'

'What's the matter?'

'I'm thinking of quitting the company.'

Kumai wasn't surprised. He'd had a feeling this day would come.

'Quit, and do what?'

'I want to become a freelance journalist.'

'You always did want to be a reporter.'

'I did. It's not that I don't enjoy the work I'm doing. And I'm grateful to you. But there's this case. I just have to become a reporter and look into it.'

'Which case?'

'The murder of an art teacher. It happened three years ago on Mt K—.'

'Is that right?' Kumai was stunned. Iwata was interested in the story that had caused him so much grief . . . But, why?

'Iwata . . . Do you have some kind of personal connection with the Mt K— case?'

'I do. The fact is, the victim, Yoshiharu Miura, was something of a mentor to me when I was a freshman.'

'A mentor?'

They'd been working together for nearly six months, and he'd had no idea. Iwata must have been avoiding the topic. Of course, it wasn't a topic that came up in casual conversation.

'I see. Was he a good teacher?'

'Well . . .'

Shunsuke Iwata

'Was he a good teacher?'

Iwata struggled to answer Kumai's question, simply because Miura hadn't actually been the type to make the grand, performative gestures people would usually expect of a 'good' teacher.

'If I'm perfectly honest, none of his students liked him. He was a stickler for the rules and for manners. He would smack students who misbehaved, and shout at those who didn't speak respectfully enough. He was the art club adviser, and I heard he was really heavy-handed in that role, too.

'But he wasn't a bad person. He was just so passionate about education that he let himself get carried away. At heart, he was very kind.

'He would spend hours talking with students about their worries, and he always took the lead in stamping out bullying. My own family situation was kind of unusual, and he helped out a lot.'

Iwata was an orphan. His mother had died when he was eleven, and his father when he was fifteen. By some terrible misfortune, both had died from illness. He had moved in with his grandfather after his father's death, but the old man's pension hadn't been enough to properly support a grandchild. So, Iwata had been forced to find part-time work while attending school. And the person who had come to Iwata's aid the most was Yoshiharu Miura.

'Iwata, you know what this is?' he'd asked one day. 'It's the Hanayagi Bento lunchbox from the supermarket in front of the station. I love them. I buy one every day. I bought a couple extra today, so why don't you take the rest home to share with your grandpa?'

And from then on, pretty much every day he'd bring two extra Hanayagi Bento boxes for Iwata and his grandfather. Thanks to him, they never went hungry despite their poverty.

Another time, Iwata had been anxious about his future and his relationships with other students and had come to Miura for advice after school. The teacher was almost certainly busy, but he still took the time to sit and talk for over two hours. In the end, he had said, with kindness in his voice, 'You know what, Iwata? I like to climb Mt K— and draw. I draw the view of the mountains from the eighth station. Next time, I'll take you with me. You'll find your cares just melt away to nothing.'

Miura could certainly be a hard teacher. He could be unreasonable and self-absorbed. But at the same time, he cared deeply for his students. If you opened yourself up to him, he would give his full attention. Iwata had wanted to go on that climbing trip with Miura. But he never got the chance.

Miura had died not long after the students had returned from their summer holidays in Iwata's first year of high school.

The news ran stories about the murder every day. And every morning, Iwata would dive into the stories as if possessed. But police failed to identify a suspect, and over time articles about the case began to dwindle, until eventually no one was talking about it at all.

He couldn't handle it. Couldn't accept that this murder would go unsolved and people would simply forget that a man named Yoshiharu Miura had ever existed. He wanted to know, more than anything. Know what had happened that day and why Miura had had to die.

When he was sixteen years old, Iwata decided to become a reporter.

Decided that, if the media wouldn't do it, he would find the truth himself.

. . . .

'So, that's it. You joined L— Daily to get a kind of vengeance for your teacher. No wonder you're frustrated working in admin.'

118

'I do like administrative work, of course. But I need to become a reporter and look into Mr Miura's case.'

'I get it. But, for someone without experience or connections, jumping into freelance reporting is going to be pretty limiting, you know. And, just saying, there's no money in it. How are you planning on making a living?'

'Um . . .'

'And then there's the most important part . . . The way I see it, you're not cut out to be a reporter.'

'What? Why would you say that?!'

'You're too soft.'

That comment sent Iwata into a rage. 'Stop it, Kumai! Don't make fun of me! I'm serious about this!'

'Then why aren't you interviewing me?'

'. . . What do you mean?'

'I was a reporter here up until three years ago. Didn't you know that?'

'Yes.'

'Well, I never mentioned this before, but at the time, I was the lead reporter on the Mt K— murder.'

'You were? Really?!'

'Yeah. That means I've got a mountain of material on the case. And I've been right beside you the whole time. Why didn't you start asking me about my stories the minute you found out I used to be a reporter?'

'I guess it was because . . .'

'Because I'm your boss? You're going to hold back just because I'm your superior? That's how I know you're soft. The first thing you do is you find someone who might have a lead and you grab onto them, no matter who, boss or not.

That's what a reporter does. If you tried to go freelance right now, you'd starve to death before you had the chance to learn anything at all.'

Iwata didn't know what to say to that.

'Iwata, listen. I'm not trying to be mean. You've got a job. If the work isn't too hard, don't quit. If you want to know about the case, I'll tell you. Hold on a minute.'

Kumai pulled a thick folder out of his desk drawer.

The cover read 'Mt K— art teacher murder (1992), investigation materials'.

'I had my own ideas about this case. I couldn't let it go, even after I stopped being a reporter. Now, I'm glad I kept this.'

'Will you let me see it?'

'Yeah. Just don't tell anyone.'

'Of course.'

'And . . . You'd best be prepared. There's a lot of detail in there about exactly how Yoshiharu Miura was murdered. I imagine it's not really something you're dying to read.'

Television reports at the time often mentioned that Miura's murder had been a brutal one, but Iwata had never learned in detail how he had died. In all honesty, if it could be avoided, he would rather not know the details of his mentor's demise. But he was the one who'd decided he wanted to 'reveal the truth'. He gulped.

'Iwata, you sure you're ready?'

'. . . Yeah.'

'All right, then. Let's open it up.'

.   .   .

Kumai pointed out facts in the documents as he outlined the case.

'Miura had planned a camping trip to Mt K— from the twentieth to the twenty-first of September 1992.'

SUNDAY	MONDAY
20	21
Off	Founding Day holiday

'The twentieth was a Sunday. And, as you know from your student days, the twenty-first was the school's founding day holiday. So, he was taking advantage of the three-day weekend. However, some work came up on Sunday morning.'

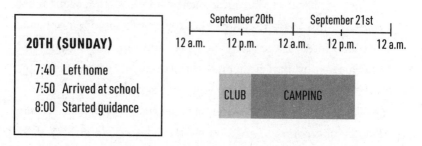

20TH (SUNDAY)

7:40 Left home
7:50 Arrived at school
8:00 Started guidance

September 20th — September 21st
12 a.m. 12 p.m. 12 a.m. 12 p.m. 12 a.m.

CLUB CAMPING

'He had to watch over a session of the art club. It seems he decided to go ahead with his camping trip once that was over.'

'Sunday morning, Miura left at seven forty and drove to the school. He had his hiking pack in the car. According to his wife, the pack contained camping equipment like a simple tent, a sleeping bag, a pocket torch and water. He also had a sketchbook and pencils for drawing.'

'He arrived at school at seven fifty. He went straight to the art room without stopping by the staffroom. He was there to advise a junior, a young woman named Kameido, one-on-one.'

'One-on-one? I thought it was an art club?'

'It seems that Miura was so harsh, the art club had hardly any members.'

'Oh . . . Now that you mention it, I think I did hear something about that. Like, they had ten new people sign up, but they all left in the first month.'

'Right. At the time, there were zero freshmen, and only one sophomore. The only junior was Kameido herself.'

'An art club with two members . . . Wow.'

'And that day, the sophomore was off for a relative's funeral. So, Kameido was alone.'

'Wouldn't they normally cancel any activities in that situation?'

'Yes. But because Miura was such a hard head, they went ahead anyway. "Just get on with it. You don't need anyone else!" and all that. I interviewed Kameido once, and she really did not like Miura. He must have been pretty hard on her. My notes from that interview are in here, too, so you can read for yourself.'

'What about him? If I'm honest, I didn't much care for him. Actually, I quite disliked him. . . . No, I'm not the only one. Hardly any of the students at school actually liked Mr Miura. He was so quick to anger. . . . He probably thought of himself as some kind of passionate educator or whatever, but honestly, we all thought he was a pain. He yelled at me all the time when he was giving me guidance for the club . . . It really scared me. . . .'

'By the way, Miura mentioned to Kameido that he was planning to go camping that afternoon during their session.'

. . .

'The club activity finished at one in the afternoon. Miura immediately went to his car and headed to the station.

'The nearest station was between the school and Mt K—. He could have gone directly to the mountain, but Miura had some errands to run near the station. One was to go to the **station-front supermarket to buy lunch**, and the other was **to pick up a man living nearby, name of Toyokawa**.'

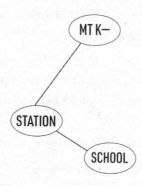

'Toyokawa? Who is that?'

'A friend of Miura's from art school. Well, I use the word "friend" since Toyokawa admitted himself that he actually didn't like Miura much at all.'

'Yoshiharu and I have been friends since our art school days. He looked out for me after we graduated, too. I have a weekly gig as a special lecturer for the art club at the school where he worked. . . . Of course, he got me the job. I guess he was worried about me working some minimum-wage part-time thing. He said I should get a second job to help pay the bills. I mean, I'm grateful and all. I was grateful but . . . Well.

If you ask how much I liked the guy . . . it's not so simple. He tended to do just do what he wanted and expected me to go along. He'd call me up and say, "Let's go hiking tomorrow!" or "Let's go for a drink!" without even considering I might have other plans.'

'The evening before, meaning Saturday, it seems Miura called up Toyokawa and said, "Let's you and me go camping on Mt K— tomorrow to Monday!" Toyokawa ordinarily would have said yes, but apparently this time he refused. And of course he had to. As a company man, he wouldn't have Monday off, and he'd have to be there in the morning, like most everyone else. He wouldn't be able to spend the night camping. But Miura didn't give up, even when Toyokawa told him that.'

'He didn't?'

'No. He had a counter-offer. Toyokawa could accompany him halfway up the mountain, then head back down that evening.'

'Accompany him halfway . . . That comes across as kind of pushy.'

'So, Toyokawa ended up following Miura's suggestion and made a day trip of it. They met up in front of the station, swung by the supermarket and bought lunch to eat on the mountain. Miura bought a sweet bun, a pork cutlet sandwich and the shop's Hanayagi Bento lunch.'

'After they had bought their lunch, they took Miura's car to the mountain, arriving at half past one. They parked in the car park at the base of the

20TH (SUNDAY)	
7:40	Left home
7:50	Arrived at school
8:00	Started guidance
13:00	Left school
13:10	Met Toyokawa at station, shopping
13:30	Arrived at mountain, began hike

mountain and started their hike. By the way, Iwata, have you ever gone up Mt K—?'

'Once. A long time ago, with my father, we went up to the fourth station. It was an easy enough hike, even for a kid like me.'

'That's right. I hiked it plenty of times in the course of researching this story. It's a gentle slope and pretty easy. The trails are marked with rope so you can't get lost, and they're even paved part of the way up. So, it's a popular spot with locals, and you run into people all along the trail. There's one more reason it's popular, though.

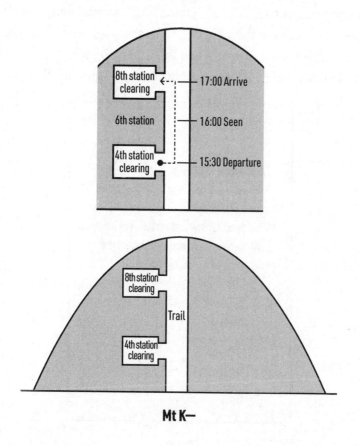

Mt K—

125

'There are wide open rest areas at the fourth and eighth stations, and the fourth station even has tables set up so it's ideal for picnics. The eighth station is good for camping, too.'

'Around half past two, Miura and Toyokawa reached the fourth station rest area and had lunch. Miura ate the **Hanayagi Bento** from the supermarket. Remember that. It's important. After they ate, the two drew pictures in the clearing before splitting up at around half past three. Toyokawa headed down the mountain, and Miura set out for the eighth station.'

'From this point, several people coming down the mountain report seeing Miura. The last sighting was at **around four, near the sixth station**. Now, the trail gets a bit steeper after the sixth station, and it takes at least an hour to get from there to the eighth. So, we can assume Miura reached the eighth station **sometime after five**.'

20TH (SUNDAY)

7:40	Left home
7:50	Arrived at school
8:00	Started guidance
13:00	Left school
13:10	Met Toyokawa at station, shopping
13:30	Arrived at mountain, began hike
14:30	Arrived at fourth station
	Lunch and sketching
15:30	Split with Toyokawa, restarted hike
16:00	Last seen near sixth station

21ST (MONDAY)

9:00	Body discovered

'And then we come to nine o'clock the next morning. A man discovers Miura's body lying in the clearing of the eighth station.'

'Why was that man climbing so early in the morning?'

'He's a **caretaker on Mt K—**. He'd heard there'd been some damage to amenities around the eighth station, so he went to check.'

'Like I said, the trails up Mt K— are marked with rope. The day before, meaning Sunday, it appears some college kids were playing around, jumping off the posts supporting the ropes, and broke one of them.'

'That was reckless of them.'

'Yeah, but it seems they felt bad about it after they got down and called the caretaker's office to apologize. It was already after ten in the evening when they called, so he went up early the next morning to check and had the bad luck to discover Miura. A sad story . . .'

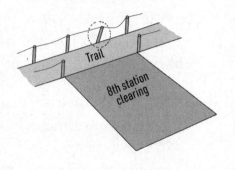

'*On the morning of the twenty-first, I hiked up to check for damage on the mountain trail. Then I saw someone on the ground . . . I'm sorry. I feel sick just thinking about it. Anyway, he was in a terrible state. . . . Yes, I came down the mountain immediately and contacted the police.*'

'The caretaker came down and called the police. They began investigating the scene from around noon. They found Miura's ID in his pack and his car parked at the foot of the mountain, so they assumed the remains were Miura's.'

'Only assumed?'

'They couldn't make a positive identification on the spot. The body was in too bad a state. The face was so disfigured, they couldn't even tell if it was a man or woman, much less match it to his ID. It sounds gruesome, but the remains were barely identifiable as human.'

'Oh no. That's horrible.'

'I understand there were stab wounds as well as signs he was struck with a rock over two hundred times.'

'Two hundred . . .'

'When a murder is that brutal, it is usually for one of two reasons. The first is to make it impossible to identify the body. The second is to satisfy a deep, terrible grudge. In this case, which one do you think it was?'

'If the goal had been to keep anyone from identifying the body, it's odd they didn't remove his ID from the scene. So, it must have been a grudge . . . Right?'

'Exactly. The murderer must have really hated Miura.'

Iwata felt a chill. Hatred strong enough to batter a body with a rock over two hundred times. What could have happened between Miura and his murderer?

.   .   .

'So, when was Mr Miura murdered?'

'They actually have a pretty good idea. The body was so badly damaged that it made the autopsy difficult, I guess, but luckily they did find partially digested food in the stomach. It was apparently the grocery store's Hanayagi Bento.'

'Food takes about three hours to be digested in the stomach. Once it's finished, the stomach empties itself. If you die in the

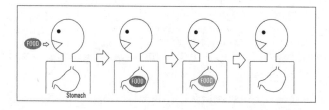

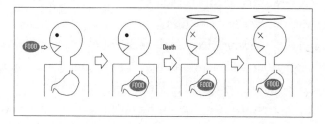

meantime, the stomach stops working, and any food remains in the stomach. So, examining the level of digestion of the food helped reveal the time of death. Miura's death was determined to be roughly two and a half hours after his last meal. Miura ate the Hanayagi Bento at around half past two . . . So, he must have died at around five o'clock.'

'I see. Wait, though. You just said that he must have arrived at the eighth station at five or later.'

'Right. Meaning, Miura must have been murdered almost immediately upon reaching the station.'

13:00	Left school
13:10	Met Toyokawa at station, shopping
13:30	Arrived at mountain, began hike
14:30	Arrived at fourth station Lunch and sketching
15:30	Split with Toyokawa, restarted hike
16:00	Last seen near sixth station
17:00	(roughly) Arrived at eighth station, attacked soon after

21ST (MONDAY)

9:00	Body discovered

'So, now, Iwata, having heard all this, does it give you any ideas about the murderer?'

'Let's see . . . First, thinking about the state of the body, the murderer must have truly hated Mr Miura. So, I think that must mean **the murderer knew him.**'

'I agree. Sometimes two people meet for the first time and end up in a fight that leads to murder . . . It's rare but it does happen. But you wouldn't expect a killer like that to batter a body over two hundred times. Yes, the murderer knew him. And I'd say knew him well.'

'It must also have been someone who knew he was hiking up the mountain on Sunday. So, from the people we've heard from so far, the primary suspects would be **Mr Miura's wife, Kameido**, from the art club and **Toyokawa**.'

'Exactly. Naturally, there were other people who fitted those criteria, but based solely on their closeness to the victim, the police focused on those three. Then, after they checked their alibis, they settled on one key suspect.'

'They did?!'

'I'll take things in order. Setting aside Toyokawa, who left Miura at the fourth station, we'll examine the other two suspects' alibis. To get from their respective neighbourhoods to station eight on Mt K— takes a good three hours one-way, even with public transport.'

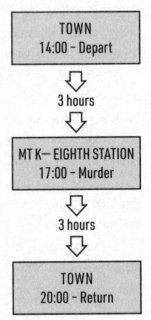

130

'If we assume the murder took place at five . . . Given the round-trip time, then they'd be in the clear with an alibi from two to eight o'clock.'

'Right, but we have one more clue. Some of the equipment Miura packed had gone missing: **his sleeping bag, the sweet bun and the cutlet sandwich**. Remember, he bought the last two along with his bento at the station-front supermarket. He'd probably planned on having them for dinner and breakfast. But then he was murdered before he had the chance. The autopsy turned up no trace of them in his stomach. That's a pretty good hint that **the murderer took them from the scene**.'

'Hmm . . . Taking food and a sleeping bag . . . It sounds like the murderer planned on spending the night on the mountain, then climbing down the next morning.'

'That's what you'd think. But it's still odd. Miura had in his pack a lot of other supplies you'd need to spend the night outdoors, like a torch, water, a tent and such. But none of those were taken. Meaning, the murderer must have had their own. But if the murderer had brought all those with them, why would they have forgotten basic things like food and a sleeping bag?'

'Yes, when you put it like that . . . But then, why else would they have taken them?'

'I'd guess they were trying to throw the police off the scent. Look at you, right now, all caught up in the mystery of it. "The murderer spent the night on the mountain and went down in the morning." I imagine they took the food and sleeping bag to make people think exactly that. Then, they went down that same evening and made sure to have an alibi through to the next morning.'

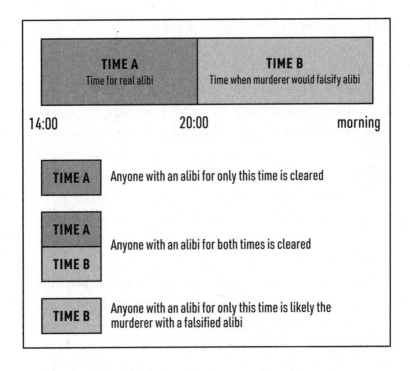

'I see! If they got the police to think the murderer stayed on the mountain, then they'd be able to clear themselves with the evening and morning alibi.'

'Right. But the police aren't that sloppy. They saw through the murderer's plan and changed their approach.'

'They designated the period of 2–8 p.m. as Time A, then from 8 p.m. to the next morning as Time B. Anyone with an alibi for Time A was cleared, while alibis for Time B were considered suspicious and actually strengthened doubt.'

'The result was, Miura's wife and Kameido were both cleared.'

'Miura's wife took their eleven-year-old son to the neighbour-hood grocer at around six in the evening on the day of the crime,

132

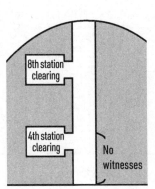

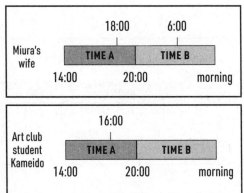

and her neighbour saw her outside working in the garden just after six the next morning. Now, as for Kameido, on the day of the crime, she said she rang her friend from her home at around four. The friend and telephone company records corroborated the story.'

'So then, Toyokawa must be the murderer.'

'That's right. The police focused their investigation on Toyokawa, and, apparently, they turned up some pretty suspicious stuff. The day of the murder, Toyokawa was supposed to have split up with Miura and headed down from the fourth station, but no one saw him on the trail down.'

'Really?'

'Right. So, there's a decent chance that Toyokawa didn't come down off the mountain at all.'

'So, he followed Mr Miura.'

'Well, no one saw him do that either. It's almost as if he simply disappeared from the fourth station. The police's theory was that, after Toyokawa said goodbye to Miura, he left the hiking trail and climbed up to the eighth station a different route.'

133

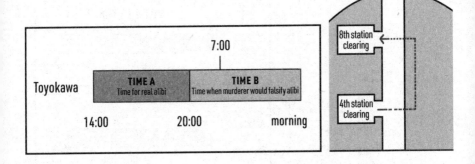

'Is there another way up?'

'Only some hidden animal trails, but apparently they're big enough for a grown man to follow easily. If he rushed, the police said, he could have reached the eighth station as fast as if he'd taken the hiking trail. So, here's how they saw it: Toyokawa left Miura but then backtracked and followed these hidden animal trails up to the eighth station. There he killed Miura, stole the food and sleeping bag, and made his way back down the mountain. Oh, and by the way, Toyokawa was up by seven the next morning exchanging greetings with his neighbours on the street outside his house.'

'So, he had an alibi for Time B . . . Making him all the more suspicious.'

From their conversation so far, it seemed Toyokawa was the only possible suspect. However . . .

'Mr Kumai . . . No one has ever been arrested for this murder. Why didn't the police take Toyokawa in?'

'They couldn't. Everything we've talked about is pure speculation. They just couldn't get enough evidence for an arrest warrant.'

'Even with all these suspicious circumstances?'

'You have to have more than suspicions. It would have been different if they had any hard evidence, but, unfortunately, not a single piece has turned up yet. And there was another problem. Toyokawa had no clear, strong motive. Sure, he didn't like Miura. But would that have been enough to drive him to brutally murder the man? It's a tough sell.'

'Were those three the only suspects?'

'I wonder about that, too. I had to give up the story and go into treatment midway through the investigation, so I don't know much more. The fact that they never made an arrest tells me they didn't have any other solid suspects, though.'

.　　.　　.

Kumai muttered to himself as he flipped through the file. 'If this was all, it would just be another bizarre murder. But there's something else strange here.'

Kumai held the file out to Iwata. On the open page were glued two photographs of drawings.

'What's that?'

'There was a sketchbook in the pack Miura left at the crime scene. There were several drawings in it, and

135

these photos show two of them. They were both presumably drawn at the fourth station on the day of the crime.'

'OK, but what's strange about them?'

'These aren't what's strange. That would be Miura's final picture, drawn at the eighth station.'

'There's a final picture?'

Kumai turned to the next page. Iwata looked closely at the photo glued to it.

It was a drawing, crudely done, far too crudely for a skilled artist like Miura.

'Did he really draw this?'

'Yeah, that is definitely his work. It seems to be the view out over the mountains from the eighth station. As I'm sure you remember, Mt K— is right on the edge of the range, near the outskirts of the city. When you get up to the eighth station, you can see the mountain range stretching off in the distance. Miura apparently loved that view. He sketched it many times before he died.'

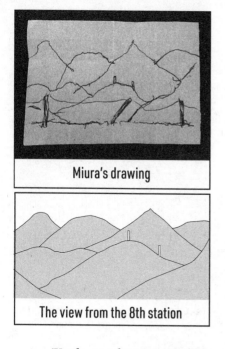

Miura's drawing

The view from the 8th station

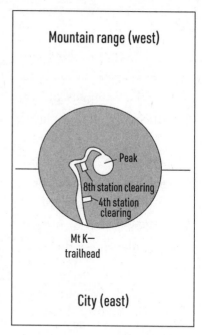

Mountain range (west)

Peak

8th station clearing

4th station clearing

Mt K—
trailhead

City (east)

'You know what, Iwata? I like to climb Mt K— and draw. I draw the view of the mountains from the eighth station.'

'I remember Mr Miura telling me something about that. But . . . This picture . . .'

'It's weird, right? It has none of the finesse of the others. And it was drawn on the back of a receipt.'

.   .   .

'Miura's wallet was in his trouser pocket. The police found this receipt in it. It's from the supermarket where he bought food on Sunday. And this picture was drawn on the back. The crime lab determined from prints and such that Miura drew it himself using a ballpoint pen that he usually kept in his pocket. It's rough, but I don't get the feeling that he did it carelessly. I climbed up to the eighth station and looked at the scenery myself, and the drawing is more or less accurate.'

'The height, slope and position of each mountain, even the antennas on top of them, are all reproduced faithfully. He must have really wanted to get them right. It even has grid lines.'

'What do you mean?'

'Look closely at the picture. You can see the folds, right?'

'Ah, you're right. Those fine lines, like it's been folded.'

'I'm not much of an artist so I didn't know this myself, but apparently it's quite common to draw over grid lines, to keep your drawing accurate and in proportion.'

'So, Mr Miura made grid lines on this receipt by folding it?'

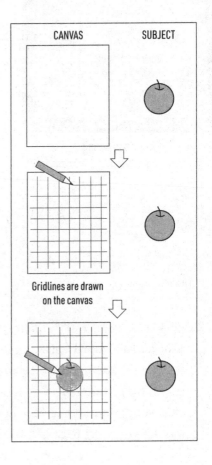

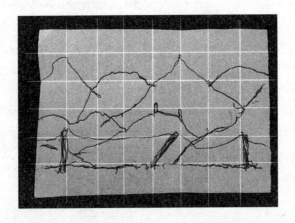

'That's what the police thought, anyway. And if you look closely, you can see how the drawing follows the gridlines.'

'But why did he draw on the back of a receipt?'

'Exactly. If he wanted to draw, why not use the sketchbook? But the fact remains, he didn't. Why do you think that is?'

The question made Iwata consider a chilling possibility.

'Because . . . He was in no condition to get to his sketchbook?'

'Right. This is what I think happened. Miura reached the eighth station, and then he was attacked and stabbed. Then, for some reason, the attacker backed off for a time, and during that respite, Miura took out the receipt and ballpoint, his hands trembling with fear, and drew the scenery behind his attacker. The mountains, I mean. He put the picture away, and soon after, the attacker brutally murdered him.'

That certainly explained the picture being drawn on the back of a receipt, but it strained credulity. Why would Miura, faced with a knife-wielding criminal, draw a picture rather than run away?

Then, Iwata thought of another possibility. 'Mr Kumai, do you really think he drew the picture when he was on the verge of death?'

'What do you mean?'

'Mr Miura had visited the eighth station many times. Maybe he just happened to have a picture he'd drawn before in his wallet.'

'Not a chance. Didn't I tell you? The receipt he drew on was from when he bought lunch at the supermarket that day.'

'Oh, right.'

'And look at the picture again. There are three posts standing in the foreground, right? Those are the posts holding the trail

139

marker rope. And can you see how the one in the middle is leaning over?'

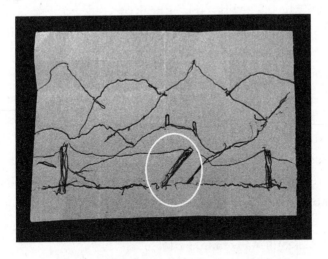

'What? Oh! Is that . . . ?'

'You remember, right? How those college climbing club kids were messing around and broke one of the posts at the eighth station. It was just a few hours before Miura was killed.'

'So, the picture must have been drawn just before he died.'

'Right. In the short period of time between when he reached the eighth station and when he was killed.'

So, he drew a picture of mountain scenery while he was being attacked. Why on earth did he do it?

'Could this picture be some kind of clue? A message, identifying the killer?'

'I wonder. If so, I wish he'd just drawn the murderer's face. Of course, if he had, I guess they'd have got rid of the picture anyway.'

'Right.'

Perhaps Miura had encoded the message in the picture

somehow, so the murderer wouldn't see it and get rid of the drawing. But, even so, why had the murderer left it behind? OK, so Miura hadn't drawn his attacker's face or written down their name, but if their victim had drawn a weird picture before he died, wouldn't the killer have got rid of it just in case?

As Iwata sat in thought, Kumai said, 'Anyway, that's the case in a nutshell. It's getting late. I'm heading home.'

. . .

Iwata headed back to his company dorm and lay down in his drab, eight-mat room. He couldn't get Miura's drawing out of his head. It was the grid lines that were bothering him the most.

There were no such lines behind the pictures Miura had drawn in his sketchbook. That told him that, normally, Miura was **not the type to use grid lines when drawing**. So, why then had he been so careful to include them in that picture of the mountains? Did he have a particular reason for wanting the picture to be accurate?

The more he thought about it, the more confused he felt.

Iwata gave a little sigh and rolled over in bed. His eyes

came to rest on the calendar on the wall. It was almost September. The third anniversary of Miura's death was approaching.

'You know what, Iwata? I like to climb Mt K— and draw. I draw the view of the mountains from the eighth station.'

Maybe I should try climbing next month.

Iwata thought he would like to see for himself the scenery that Miura had so loved.

.   .   .

THREE SUSPECTS

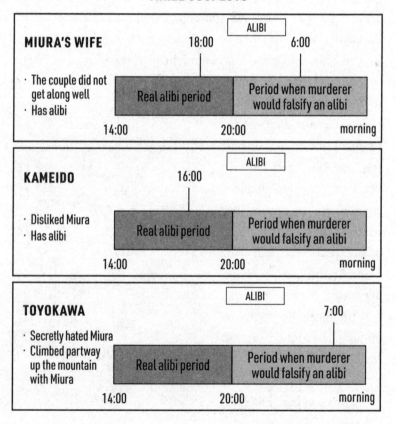

MIURA'S MOVEMENTS ON THE DAY OF THE MURDER

20TH (SUNDAY)

 7:40 Left home
 7:50 Arrived at school
 8:00 Started guidance
13:00 Left school
13:10 Met Toyokawa at station, shopping
13:30 Arrived at mountain, began hike
14:30 Arrived at fourth station
       Lunch and sketching
15:30 Split up from Toyokawa, restarted hike
16:00 Last seen near sixth station
17:00 (roughly) Arrived at eighth station, drew picture on back of receipt
       Killed soon after

21ST (MONDAY)

 9:00 Body discovered

- Body sustained over 200 injuries → Terrible grudge?
- Stolen sleeping bag and food → Faked alibi?
- Mountain picture on back of receipt → Why?

On his lunch break the next day, Iwata sat at his desk over his open notebook. In it, he had written out a summary of what Kumai had told him and the details of the case. No matter how you looked at it, Toyokawa was the most obvious suspect. But there was no hard evidence, and Kumai insisted his motive was too weak.

Motive . . . Iwata had been thinking about that the night before. Couldn't Toyokawa have harbored some other, deeper resentment buried in his heart? Miura and he had known each other since art school. They'd been something like friends for over twenty years. Over that time, perhaps some kind of darker feeling towards Miura had taken root in Toyokawa, and grown, slowly but surely. It was certainly a possibility, wasn't it?

He wanted to hear what Toyokawa had to say. To interview him.

Just about then, Kumai came up behind him and clapped him on the shoulder.

'Keen, aren't you?'

'I put together everything you told me yesterday.'

'I see that. So, how about what you told me? Still quitting your job?'

'Oh, that. I think I'll keep at it a bit longer.'

'I think that's a good idea. These days, there's no sense throwing away a good salary. You can go freelance anytime. There's no rush.'

'About that. Is it all right for me to follow up on reporting work on my days off?'

'Come again?'

'I won't cause any trouble for the paper. I really just want to follow up on Mr Miura's case as a personal thing, outside of work.'

'Follow up, you say? What exactly are you planning on doing?'

'I want to interview Toyokawa. Find out what he really thought about Mr Miura. I want to ask him directly and uncover his true motive.'

Kumai thought for a moment.

'I doubt there'll be any trouble as long as the publisher doesn't find out,' he said, a serious expression on his face. "But I'm against it.'

'Why, if I may ask?'

'Listen. He was never arrested, but Toyokawa is most likely the murderer. If you waltz up to him and say, "I'm looking into this case. Did you hate the victim?" he's going to get nervous about people digging up dirt, and that could put you in real danger.'

'Oh.'

'Reporting can be a dangerous business. So, we all learn ways to protect ourselves. But it's not easy. You need experience, Iwata, and you don't have any as a reporter at all. You're barely an adult. You shouldn't be taking these kinds of risks.'

'I understand. But still . . .'

'Ah, well. I guess you're dead set on talking to Toyokawa, but why not just make it a chat?'

'What do you mean, a chat?'

'Toyokawa used to work as an outside lecturer for the art club every Saturday on Miura's word. There's a chance he's still doing the work. And you're an alumnus, right? What's suspicious about a former student coming to visit the old alma mater? So, get in touch with Toyokawa as just another person, not a reporter. Make up some reason for meeting him. And then you can ferret out some details in a nice, casual chat.'

'I see.'

'Interviews are just conversations, when you get down to it. So, try starting with a conversation.'

'I get it. Thank you!'

.   .   .

The next Saturday, Iwata rode the train for thirty minutes and got off at the station nearest his old school. When he was a student, he had taken the bus every day from his grandfather's house, so he'd hardly ever used this station. But still, the feel of the streets was the same as he walked towards the school.

The old familiar wooden school building came in sight after about fifteen minutes. He could hear the shouts of some sports team practising on the field. He hadn't visited once during the six months since he'd graduated. He stopped by the office for a visitor's pass and slippers, then headed to the staffroom.

As he walked down the corridors, the classrooms, toilets, stairwells . . . they all looked the same. But Iwata felt somehow uncomfortable. This place, where just six months before he had walked without care, now felt like another world. The chill air of the building seemed to reject him, saying, 'You no longer belong here any more.'

But Iwata was welcomed warmly in the staffroom. Several of his old teachers came rushing over.

'Iwata! Good to see you again! How've you been?'

'I heard you joined a newspaper! So, are you a reporter now?'

'Really? Is he going to press conferences and everything now?'

He smiled and fended off the questions as he made his way towards a desk in the depths of the office where a teacher sat working. It was Ms Maruoka, who had taken over as art teacher after Miura's murder. He'd heard that she was also the art club adviser.

With her permed hair and overalls, she had an unusual look for a schoolteacher, but her easy-going character made her popular with students, who affectionately called her 'Miss Maru'. He'd never talked to her outside of art class, but he still remembered her as a strong and distinctive character.

'Hello, Ms Maruoka. It's good to see you again. I'm Shunsuke Iwata. I was in your art class until last year.'

'Oh! Hi there! I heard everyone making a fuss just now. So, you're a reporter these days?'

'Not a reporter, no, but I do work at the newspaper.'

'Well, isn't that something! So, what brings you by today?'

'There's something I wanted to ask you. I think a man named Toyokawa used to be an outside lecturer for the art club. Is he still doing that?'

'Nope. He quit. Quite a while ago.'

Too late . . . Iwata slumped in disappointment.

'Can you tell me why he quit?'

'I understand that he had to move because his full-time employer transferred him.'

'Do you know where he moved to?'

'Hmm . . . Sorry, I can't recall. Oh, but Kame might know.'

'Kame?'

'She's the outside lecturer who took over after Toyokawa quit. A young girl.'

'Could you mean Kameido, who used to be in the art club?'

'Oh, you know her? That's right. She's still in art school, but she comes by every week for a bit of part-time work. She's supervising an activity right now. I think they're about done. Would you like to talk to her?'

'Yes, please!'

It was an unexpected coincidence. His plans for Toyokawa were a bust, but he was lucky to have found someone else involved in the case. They headed towards the art room, Maruoka in the lead. The art club members were shuffling out of the classroom as they approached. It seemed the activity was over.

Now that Miura's strict supervision was a thing of the past, the club membership seemed to have grown. The students called out to Maruoka as they passed with variations on, 'Hey Miss Maru!' and 'Bye, now!'

'Yes, yes, good job everyone. Take care getting home.'

They talked more like friends than students and teacher. If a student had talked to Miura like that, he'd have sat them down for an hour's lecture at least. Iwata couldn't help a strained smile.

Inside the classroom, a young woman was busy washing paint brushes. Maruoka called out to her:

'Kame! This young reporter wants to talk to you!' He tried to correct her but Maruoka talked over him. 'All right, then, I'll leave you two to talk,' she said and did just that.

A tension filled the air as soon as they were left alone in the room. Kameido stared at Iwata suspiciously. Which was understandable, given this surprise visit from a 'reporter' looking to talk to her. Iwata forced a gentle smile onto his face, hoping to encourage her to lower her guard.

'Ms Kameido, I am very sorry for showing up all of a sudden. My name is Shunsuke Iwata. I graduated from here.'

'You were a student at this school?'

'I was. I do work at a newspaper now, but I'm not here to interview you or anything. I just want to ask you something, personally. Do you have a few minutes?'

'Yes, I suppose. Have a seat over here for now.'

The two sat across from each other at a large wooden table. Looking at her up close like this, he could see just how pretty a girl she was. Her large eyes sparkled, and her skin was so pale as to be almost translucent. Her dark hair was gathered up in back, but if she let it down, it looked like it would be quite long. With the two-year gap between them, they'd never met before, but Iwata found himself shocked that such a beautiful woman had been at the same school as him.

'What I want to ask you, Ms Kameido, is about the man who used to teach here, a Mr Toyokawa. Do you know him?'

'Yes, he taught here every week when I was a student.'

'I heard that he had to move because of his full-time job. Would you know where it was he moved to?'

'I think I heard he was moving to Fukui Prefecture, but I'm afraid I don't know any other details. Um, do you need something from Mr Toyokawa?'

'Well, yes. There's something I want to ask him about.'

'Is it . . . Is it about Mr Miura?'

Iwata sat up in shock.

Of course. If you heard that someone from a newspaper was looking into Toyokawa, you would naturally make the connection to the Miura murder. But there was something else in Kameido's expression and voice. Iwata thought it would be better to come clean with her, rather than try to make up some excuse.

'Yes. Honestly, Mr Miura was something of a mentor to me.'

'Oh.'

'Now, I'm looking into his death for personal reasons. I came here hoping today to talk directly with Mr Toyokawa, since he was involved in the case.'

'I see . . .'

'Ms Kameido, if you know anything about Toyokawa, anything at all, would you tell me? Please?'

'I . . . I'm not sure if I should say this.' Kameido spoke quietly, as if worried about being overheard. 'I . . . **I think Mr Toyokawa killed Mr Miura.**'

He was taken aback hearing his own suspicions from her lips.

'Why do you think that?'

'I felt like Toyokawa . . . must have hated Mr Miura terribly.'

'Terribly?'

'Yes. I only found out about this after the murder. At the time, I was taking design lessons every Saturday from Mr Toyokawa, but after Mr Miura died, Mr Toyokawa started to say nasty things about him during our lessons. Things like, "You'd best forget everything Miura ever taught you," or "That man was just some dull public employee, he had no talent at all" and so on. Speaking ill of the dead.'

'I've not heard that before. I did know that Toyokawa thought Mr Miura was self-centred and irritating. But why would he deny Miura's artistic talent?'

'The reason for that goes back a long way. Apparently Mr Toyokawa was a talented artist from his childhood. He was an elite student who got into art school with top marks and was even asked to give the speech at their entrance ceremony. Meanwhile, Mr Miura barely scraped in, just a few spots above the bottom rank. He used to joke about it himself, before his death. They were in the same year, but as I understand it, Toyokawa used to coach Miura in drawing. Their relationship was more that of master and apprentice than of classmates.'

'I never knew any of that.'

'That dynamic flipped when they graduated, though. Mr Toyokawa got a job with a Tokyo design firm, but he apparently couldn't handle the workload and even got into fights with the other employees. He ended up quitting after a few years. When he had trouble finding a new position, Mr Miura offered to help him out and got him a second job teaching the art club. I imagine the idea of having to accept help from someone he used to tutor was hard to swallow for someone as proud as Mr Toyokawa . . . Or, at least, that's what I think now. That's just a guess, though, I'm afraid.'

'Not at all, it's quite helpful. I have to say, you sound like you know Toyokawa quite well. Did you spend time with him outside of art club, too?'

'Yes . . . I used to see him when I had dinner at Mr Miura's house, actually.'

'At Miura's house? Really?'

'Yes. And I began to stop by after his death rather a lot. I thought his widow would have so much to deal with with her husband gone and everything, so I went to lend a hand with the cooking and watch their son. Just to help out, really.'

That struck Iwata as odd. Miura had certainly given Kameido a lot of guidance in the art club, but how many students would go to such lengths to help a dead teacher's family? And hadn't Kameido said she disliked Miura himself?

'Anyway,' Kameido went on, 'Mr Toyokawa would often visit at the same time as me. He'd always bring something for dinner, like meat or fish.'

'Really? So, even though he insulted Mr Miura's memory, he did his best for the man's family.'

'Not exactly . . . I think he had something else in mind.'

'Such as?'

'I saw Mr Toyokawa making advances on Mrs Miura quite a few times. He always had this disgusting look in his eyes.'

'You did?!'

'I did. Mrs Miura looked so frightened every time it happened . . . And I had no idea what to do.'

Toyokawa's vulgar character was becoming clear. But even as Iwata's suspicion of the man grew stronger, he also began to have doubts about Kameido.

'Thank you for this valuable information, Ms Kameido. There's just one last thing I want to ask you. What did you think of Mr Miura?'

'What do you mean?'

'At the time, you told the newspaper you quite disliked Mr Miura. But even so, you went to help his family . . . You worried about his wife . . . Why would you do all that?'

Kameido dropped her eyes and started fidgeting. She said:

'I . . . loved him.'

'What . . . ?'

'I loved Mr Miura. But I wasn't lying when I said I disliked him. He lost his temper with me all the time, and there was a lot I didn't like about him. But no one else was as kind to me as he was.'

The totally unexpected words continued to spill from her lips.

'My parents don't get along. They just ignore each other. I suppose that's why Mr Miura was so hard on me, because he felt some kind of parental responsibility for me. I rebelled, though, and there were times when I just couldn't stand him. But when he died . . . it was so painful, it felt like I'd lost a part of my body. I couldn't stop crying for days. I think . . . Maybe part of me felt something more for him.'

'You mean, you were in love with him?'

'I suppose I must have been. But I was embarrassed about it and didn't want anyone to know. I was trying to deny it when

152

I told the interviewer I didn't like him. Otherwise, I thought all those other emotions would overflow and I would just lose control. Even now, whenever I think about him . . .'

Kameido's face was flushed, and she suddenly burst into tears. Iwata was stunned. But, at the same time, he felt somehow . . . validated?

He recalled how, when Miura died, none of his fellow students had cried. Perhaps that reflected badly on Yoshiharu Miura as a teacher. One classmate had even remarked, 'I'm glad the old bastard is gone.' No one had agreed, or not out loud at least. But Iwata suspected that many of the other students felt the same way.

Iwata had felt so alone. Like he was the only person in the whole world to be mourning Miura's death. But now, with Kameido sitting there weeping in front of him, he had finally found a kindred spirit.

'Ms Kameido, thank you for speaking with me today. Mr Miura looked out for me, too. It feels good to meet someone who misses him like I do.'

'Yes, likewise.'

'Oh, one other thing. The truth is, I'm planning on climbing Mt K— on the twentieth of this month. I was thinking it would be a kind of memorial to him on the day of his death. If you have the time, would you like to come with me?'

'Thank you. But I have a class I can't get out of that day.'

'Ah. That's too bad.'

'I'm sorry. It was kind of you to invite me. Um . . . If you do the same thing next year, please let me join you then.'

'Yes, of course! Right, let me give you my card. Get in touch if anything happens.'

'Thank you. Shall I give you mine?'

'A student with a business card?'

'Yeah, we made them as a project for college. They're kind of embarrassing, but . . . Here.'

The card Kameido handed him had a delightful design.

Next to a colourful drawing of flowers, her name was written out in kanji and the Roman alphabet.

亀戸由紀

Yuki Kameido

Iwata thanked her and rose from his chair.

When he did, he suddenly noticed a single picture in the corner of the room—a painting of a cat, propped on a wooden easel. For some reason, the canvas was covered in tiny holes.

'Ms Kameido, what is that painting?'

'Oh! I bet you're wondering about the holes. They let you draw on the canvas without seeing it.'

'You don't need to see?'

'That's right. There's a blind girl in our art club, and Ms Maruoka came up with this idea for her. Have you ever tried drawing with your eyes closed?'

PIERCED CANVAS

NORMAL CANVAS

Can sense location by touch to maintain proportions when drawing

Cannot draw without seeing

'No, I suppose I haven't.'

'If you've ever played pin the tail on the donkey, you know how hard it is to do things when you can't see your hands. Pictures are particularly difficult, because how do you know where to draw a line if you can't see the canvas? But if you put holes in the canvas, you can find your position by touch, and use that to guide the drawing.

'So, for example, if you connect the bottom left point, the bottom right point, and the top middle point, you can make a triangle. Even if you can't see, you can transfer the idea in your head onto the canvas. We've been using the system to allow the girl to learn to draw all kinds of things, people or animals even.'

'I see. So it's possible to draw by your sense of touch alone . . .'

And then it was like a flash of lightning ran through Iwata's brain.

The canvas full of holes reminded him of something that had been niggling at him this whole time.

Those folds in the paper Miura used for his drawing. Couldn't they serve the same purpose as the holes?

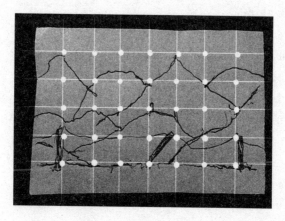

155

Folding the paper had made points of reference on the paper at the intersections of the folds. That's why Miura had folded it, not to create guidelines. The principle was exactly the same as that behind the canvas full of holes Maruoka had made for the blind art club member. **It was a way to draw a picture blind.**

So, if he was right, then Miura had drawn the picture on the receipt blind, too.

But there was still something odd about that idea.

If he had been blinded, say, by the murderer covering his eyes, that would also mean **he wouldn't have been able to see the mountains, so he couldn't have drawn them**. At the very least, Miura must have been able to see the view out over the mountain range. So, if he couldn't see his hands . . . What could have been going on?

Iwata mulled it over, and finally arrived at an explanation.

Could his hands have been tied behind his back?

The murderer tied Mr Miura up. With his hands tied behind his back, Miura had managed to get the receipt and pen out of his pocket and draw the picture. But he couldn't see what he was doing. That's **why he folded the paper and drew the picture by touch alone.**

But Iwata still harbored some doubts.

Was it really possible for him to have drawn a picture with his hands tied behind his back?

If so, how had Miura been able to draw a whole picture without the murderer noticing?

And what had been Miura's reason for drawing the picture in such a state, anyway?

There were still too many things he didn't understand. But he felt like he finally had some kind of lead to work with.

Then came the morning of September 20th. Iwata stuffed his backpack with a newly bought tent and sleeping bag, added a sketchbook, and left his dormitory. He had initially planned on coming home that same day, but he had got two days off in a row, so he decided to make an overnight stay of it. Then he set some rules for himself.

The goal was to **recreate the day of the murder exactly**. He would take the same route as Miura, at the same time. He would see with his own eyes the same scenery that Miura had.

He arrived at the station around one in the afternoon and bought food at the supermarket. A sweet bean bun, a cutlet sandwich and a Hanayagi Bento. Then, he took a taxi to Mt K—.

Unusually for mid-September, the sun was bright enough to raise a sweat, and there were lots of people out and about. Iwata checked his watch and set out on his hike.

MIURA'S MOVEMENTS ON THE DAY OF THE MURDER

7:40 Left home
7:50 Arrived at school
8:00 Started guidance
13:00 Left school
13:10 Met Toyokawa at station, shopping
13:30 Arrived at mountain, began hike
14:30 Arrived at fourth station
        Lunch and sketching
15:30 Split with Toyokawa, restarted hike
16:00 Last seen near sixth station
17:00 (roughly) Arrived at eighth station

He climbed the gentle trail for around an hour and reached the first rest spot, the clearing at the fourth station. The six tables were already taken by other hikers, so Iwata sat at the foot of a tree and opened his bento.

'Iwata, you know what this is? It's the Hanayagi Bento lunchbox from the supermarket in front of the station. I love them. I buy one every day. I bought a couple extra today, so why don't you take the rest home to share with your grandpa?'

That's what Miura had told him, before the teacher started bringing him enough for two people every day. Sweet and sour meatballs. Big pieces of vegetable tempura. White rice topped with a pickled plum. It was the same as it had always been.

After finishing lunch, he took out the sketchbook and pencil from his pack. That day, Miura had drawn a picture here. Iwata wasn't a great artist, but if he wanted to recreate the day of the murder, he couldn't leave anything out.

He decided to start by drawing the flowers blooming at the bases of the trees. But it didn't go well. After thirty minutes, the only reward for his effort was an ugly scrawl.

'I'm just not cut out for art,' he muttered to himself as he closed the sketchbook.

A glance at his watch showed him it was twenty past three in the afternoon.

On the day of the murder, Miura had left this station at around half past. To be strict, Iwata would have to wait there another ten minutes, but he felt a little nervous about it. Unlike Miura, Iwata was not used to hiking. He hadn't been up the mountain since he was a child. There was a chance he wouldn't make it to the eighth station by five o'clock. Wouldn't it be best to leave a little room in his schedule, just to be safe? He could always slow his pace if it seemed like he would reach the next station too soon.

Iwata packed away his sketchbook and left the fourth station behind.

.   .   .

Iwata had been right.

It was already past four o'clock by the time he reached the sixth station. If he'd left the fourth station at the same time as Miura, he would have been behind schedule now. Clearly, Iwata was slower than Miura had been.

He stopped to take a drink of water, looked up at the sky and saw that it was growing faintly orange to the west. It was getting close to dusk. He'd have to hurry now, or he wouldn't make it. He set off walking faster than before.

After the sixth station, the trail became steeper. The rope markers meant there was no fear of getting lost, but the path itself was unpaved and the going was difficult. Jagged, lumpy rocks the size of rabbits rolled around underfoot, so that a moment of inattention could lead to a fall. Here and there Iwata spotted unsettling insects he'd never seen before.

Iwata walked on, trying not to lose heart. After around an hour, he finally saw a sign reading 'Eighth Station Rest Area'. He breathed a sigh of relief. It was just before five o'clock. His hurry had paid off, and he'd arrived right on time.

The rest area at the eighth station was a clearing the size of a children's play park. Unlike at the fourth station, there were no benches or other amenities, but that meant there was plenty of space to put up tents.

It was ideal for camping, but apart from Iwata the place was deserted. Hardly surprising given that it was the scene of a murder.

Iwata dropped his heavy pack to the ground and stretched his sore back.

From his pocket he took the receipt he'd got from the station-front supermarket earlier in the day. Why had Miura drawn the view from this spot just before his death? If Iwata could unravel this mystery, he might understand the message Miura had wanted to leave.

Iwata took out his pencil and looked around. This was the scenery that Miura had so loved, a beautiful view of mountains. Or, at least, that's what it was supposed be.

But what Iwata saw spreading out in front of him was hard to believe.

This . . . is wrong.

Below the sunset sky, the mountain scenery was simply a black mass.

Iwata was confused for a moment, then he understood. It was backlit.

In this season, the sun set in full at around half past five. Thirty minutes before sunset, the western sky was filled with light.

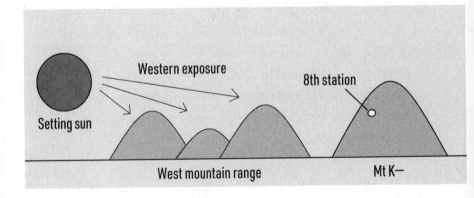

The mountain range spread out to the west of Mt K—, so that the setting sun shone from behind the mountains. So, from the eighth station of Mt K—, the **backlight** caused the range to look pitch black. In the daytime, when the mountains were lit from above, you would be able to see details on their slopes. But right now, you couldn't even tell where one mountain ended and the next began.

Iwata thought back on the picture Miura had drawn.

That picture had shown not only the outline of each mountain, but also the two antennas on one of the peaks. Any way you looked at it, there was no way Miura could have seen everything so clearly. The murder had happened three years before on this very day. The sun would have set around the same time that day. Therefore, the view should look about the same, too.

Could Mr Miura have got to the eighth station earlier, when the sun was higher in the sky?

He quashed the thought immediately. There was no way.

Iwata had left the fourth station ten minutes earlier than Miura and hurried up the mountain. Any faster and he would have been running flat out. Even as used to hiking as Miura had been, it was hard to imagine him running up the trail with a heavy pack on his back, especially since the trail was steep and unpaved after the sixth station. He would have fallen if he'd tried running up that.

He could only have got to the station at the same time as Iwata, or later.

So then how had he drawn that picture?

·   ·   ·

After a while, the sun set behind the mountains, and the world around was plunged into gloom. Iwata decided to give his thinking a break and set up camp. He put up his tent, crawled inside, turned on his lamp and took out the sweet bun and cutlet sandwich he'd bought at the supermarket.

He wondered which Miura had intended for dinner. The expiration date on the sandwich read "September 20th, 10 p.m.' Ten o'clock that evening. The sweet bun, on the other hand, was good until the next weekend. So, Miura would have had the sandwich in the evening and probably kept the longer-lasting sweet bun for breakfast the next day.

Iwata opened the quartered cutlet sandwich and ate one section. It wasn't very good. He'd heard that taste was deadened at high altitude. That was probably the reason.

He took a gulp of water to wash it down.

Just then. That was when it happened.

Something clicked in Iwata's head.

It can't be . . . Was that it?

A shock ran though his body, his heart began racing and his skin prickled into goosebumps.

The mangled body, the stolen food, the picture on the receipt . . . It connected every dot.

That's it. That's why he drew the picture of the mountains.

.   .   .

Iwata left his tent and looked to the west. The mountain range had melted into the evening dark and was now completely invisible.

But in about a dozen hours, the sun would rise again, and

the mountains would be visible once more. The police, Kumai, Iwata . . . Everyone had made a critical mistake.

Miura had drawn the mountains in the morning light.

There was only one reason he'd have drawn that picture.

'**I was alive until morning**.' That was the message he had wanted to convey.

The autopsy had placed Miura's death at around five o'clock on the twentieth of September. If he had actually been alive the next morning, that would mean the pathologist had been off in their estimate by more than ten hours. Japan's police pathologists were too good to make that kind of mistake.

But what if the murderer had used a trick to bring about that ten-hour error? Iwata thought he had spotted just such a trick.

The hint was what Kumai had told him.

'The body was so badly damaged that it made the autopsy difficult, I guess, but luckily they did find partially digested food in the stomach. It was apparently the grocery store's Hanayagi Bento. . . . So, examining the level of digestion of the food can reveal the time of death. Miura's death was determined to be roughly two and a half hours after his last meal.'

The police had placed Miura's time of death about two and a half hours after his lunch at the fourth station. But couldn't someone with some knowledge of police methods and Miura's habits have used that knowledge to fake a time of death?

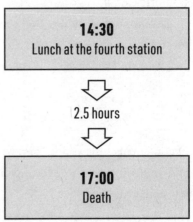

14:30
Lunch at the fourth station

2.5 hours

17:00
Death

Iwata's theory went like this:

On that day three years ago, Miura had reached the eighth station at around five o'clock, put up his tent and had something to eat—presumably the cutlet sandwich—before climbing into his sleeping bag and going to sleep. The murderer had come **after dawn the next morning**. While Miura was still groggy from sleep, the murderer had dragged him out of his tent, opened up the sleeping bag and bound his hands behind his back. Then they had **force-fed him a Hanayagi Bento they'd brought with them and washed it down with water. After that, the murderer had waited two and a half hours before killing him.**

The result was that the autopsy found that the food from the bento in Miura's stomach had only been digested for two and a half hours, which had the effect of shifting the police's estimated time of death back more than ten hours. That difference between the real and estimated times of death meant the murderer had easily been able to create an alibi for the estimated time. Anyone who knew Miura would also have known that he ate a Hanayagi Bento every day. The station-front supermarket

Around 17:00, reaches eighth station

⬇

Sets up tent, eats dinner

⬇

Crawls into sleeping bag, goes to sleep

⬇

After dawn, murderer comes to eighth station

⬇

Ties Miura up, force-feeds him the Hanayagi Bento

⬇

Later, kills him

sold them all day long, so it would have been easy for the murderer to pick one up.

It was a simple ploy. In fact, Iwata had read about it before. Force-feeding a victim to create a false time of death was an old trick used in lots of detective novels.

But . . . No, not 'but'. *Therefore*, no one had considered it in this case. It was out of the question from the start; if anyone had even suggested it the reaction would have been, 'There's no way,' or 'What kind of idiot idea is that?'

It was the kind of trick that only worked in fiction. You couldn't fool the police with something like that in the real world.

That's because the police have lots of other ways to establish time of death besides stomach contents.

One of those is rigor mortis. After death, a person's muscles begin to stiffen and then relax at a predictable rate, so measuring muscle stiffness at the time of a body's discovery can help to calculate the time of death.

There are several other ways, including measuring corneal cloudiness, the settling of blood, and so on. Analysis of stomach contents is only one method among many.

And that was it.

That was why the murderer had so thoroughly battered Miura.

The body was so badly damaged that it made the autopsy difficult, I guess, but luckily they did find partially digested food in the stomach.

In other words, the body was so badly damaged that digestion of stomach contents was the only clue the police could use to determine time of death. And that revealed the murderer's strategy.

Miura's body had been struck more than two hundred times and left so thoroughly mutilated that it was only 'something vaguely human shaped'. After that, the stomach contents were the sole remaining clue available to the pathologist. The police had mistakenly blamed the brutality of the attack on vicious hatred.

Iwata also now knew the real reason the sleeping bag had been taken.

On the night of the twentieth, Miura had set up his tent, crawled into his sleeping bag and gone to sleep. If the murderer had left the sleeping bag and tent at the crime scene, it would have been obvious that Miura had lived until morning, and the police would have quickly seen through the trick. The simple tent was easy to break down and pack away to disguise that it had been used, but there was no way to hide the traces he would have left in the sleeping bag after he'd slept in it. That was why they'd taken it away.

That was also why they'd taken the food. Miura must have eaten the sandwich on the night of the twentieth.

Even if he'd eaten it at, say, midnight, his stomach would have been empty in the morning. The autopsy would have found nothing.

But if only the sandwich had vanished from the campsite, then someone might have made the connection: Miura ate the sandwich for dinner, so he must have lived through the night. And that's why **the murderer stole the sweet bun**. With the bun missing, the police would assume the murderer had taken the cutlet too. It was all to confuse the police.

. . .

And that meant Miura must have drawn the mountain scenery to disprove the murderer's alibi.

Clearly, while the murderer was forcing the bento down his throat, he had caught on to the murderer's plan to hide the time of death. So, he'd used his bound hands to tease a pen and receipt from his pocket, and had carefully crafted a dying message that the murderer would not notice.

Miura must have considered it all so carefully. What could he draw? If he'd written the murderer's name or explained the trick and the murderer had found the paper, they'd surely have destroyed it. Instead, he had thought of a message so indirect that it might almost be missed completely. The mountain scenery.

'I survived until morning.' That is what Miura had wanted to say.

There was no way of knowing whether the murderer had found the drawing and judged that there was no danger in leaving it behind, as Miura had calculated, or whether they simply hadn't noticed it. Either way, the drawing had ended up in the hands of the police. And no one had understood its meaning.

.   .   .

So, who was the murderer?

At that time of year, sunrise was at around half past five in the morning. The body was discovered at nine. So, the murder must have taken place sometime between the two.

Given the time needed to travel to the mountain and back, Miura's wife's alibi at 6 a.m. and Toyokawa's at 7 a.m. put them in the clear. Which meant . . . There was only one possibility.

Yuki Kameido.

168

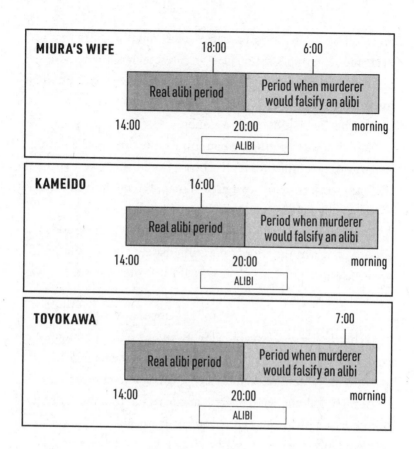

Iwata felt a chill.

He thought back to her sitting in the art room, her face stained with tears.

'I loved Mr Miura . . .'

Everything she'd said then had been a lie. What she had told Kumai in his interview had been the truth. She had hated him, so she killed him.

But perhaps not. Maybe she killed him because she loved him. That could also have been true. Love between a teacher

169

and student . . . It was forbidden. And if something like that had occurred . . . It might sound like the tritest television melodrama, but he'd heard that people's motives for murder could often be just that trivial.

But that still left one major doubt.

Kameido was a petite woman. And at the time of the murder she was only a junior in high school. Could she have managed the hard work of tying up a grown man, forcing him to eat and then brutally murdering him?

But sitting here thinking about it would do no good. He should go down the mountain immediately and tell the police what he'd learned. But . . . It was already after sunset. He was surrounded by darkness.

He didn't have the courage to hike down now.

A chill, biting wind was blowing. Evening on the mountain was cold, and the temperature would only drop further at night. Iwata got into his tent, unpacked his sleeping bag and crawled inside.

As night fell, the wind picked up and began to howl. The chaotic churring of insects echoed from all around.

He hadn't expected night on the mountain to be this unsettling. He squeezed his eyes shut, hoping for sleep to come quickly.

.   .   .

How much time had passed? He had managed to fall asleep at some point.

When he opened his eyes, it was pitch dark. Outside, the howling wind and chirping of insects went on. He tried to reach for the watch near his head to check the time.

Something was wrong, though.

He couldn't move his hands. Both arms were trapped at his sides. He couldn't move his legs either. They were stuck together.

Is this sleep paralysis?

As a child, Iwata had experienced sleep paralysis many times. But this felt somehow different.

He noticed that he could move his hands. And not only that, his head, eyes and mouth were free. Only his arms and legs were frozen.

So, not sleep paralysis. Then, what? What was happening to his body?

As he woke up fully, the sensations became clearer. He felt some kind of pressure on his arms and legs, as if they were tightly bound . . . And then Iwata understood.

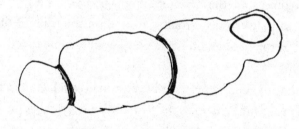

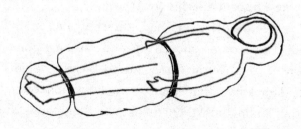

Someone had tied a rope or cord around his sleeping bag. That was the only thing he could think of. But he couldn't truly grasp it. He was at the eighth station at the top of the mountain. No one else had been around when he went to sleep.

His vision cleared as the last remnants of sleep left him, and he began to make out the interior of the tent. He moved his head around to see. When he looked down at his feet, his heart skipped a beat.

Someone was there.

Someone was sitting at his feet. He couldn't see their face, but they were small. With long hair. A woman . . . The blood froze in his body. He remembered.

He had told Yuki Kameido he would be here tonight.

Suddenly, the woman raised her arms above her head. She was holding something. Something jagged and lumpy. One of the rocks that had been rolling around on the trail. In the next instant, it came down on Iwata's legs with terrible speed.

Thunk.

With the sound came a terrible pain in his shin. Iwata's mouth gaped in a mute scream as the fear and pain strangled his voice.

The woman immediately raised her hands, and again they fell, merciless.

Thunk.

Something inside his leg made a grating sound. A bone cracking, surely. The pain took his breath away.

He resisted with all he had, thrashing his bound body around. The woman moved up and sat on him, pinning him down. And over and over, the rock came down. Thunk. Thunk. Thunkthunkthunkthunkthunkthunkthunkthunkthunk-thunkthunkthunkthunkthunkthunkthunkthunkthunkthunk.

The ceaseless agony squeezed his chest. He panted, desperately trying to get air into his lungs. The world began to grow dark as he suffocated, and finally, finally, amid the pain and the terror, he lost consciousness.

.　　.　　.

He came to. The star-filled heavens spread before him. Cold wind caressed his cheeks. He was outside. She must have dragged him out of the tent while he was unconscious.

He had to get away . . . But he couldn't move. His legs would not obey. The pain was gone. All sensation was gone. Rather than legs, they were more like heavy iron bars attached to his body.

He tried to raise his upper body instead. But he couldn't. A soft but firm weight pressed down on his chest. The woman was sitting on him.

Terror and despair filled Iwata's mind as he finally understood.

How could a petite young woman have killed Miura? **Because he was in his sleeping bag**. If you tied something like a rope around a sleeping bag, then you could completely immobilize someone with relatively little effort.

The revelation solved another riddle, too. This was how Miura had drawn the picture. His arms and legs were bound, but he was still able to use his hands to remove the pen and receipt from his pocket and desperately draw the picture inside the sleeping bag without the murderer noticing. That way, he could leave behind a message.

Then he heard a voice.

'Mr . . . Iwata, was it? I am sorry for being so terribly cruel.'

There was something odd about the voice.

It's different . . . Did Kameido sound like that?

'You didn't do anything wrong. But still . . .'

It isn't her. Kameido's voice was higher pitched, younger.

Who was this woman crouching over Iwata?

'I heard you're poking into my husband's death . . .'

Husband? It can't be . . .

And it really couldn't be. Miura's wife had an alibi for six o'clock on the morning Miura's body was discovered. There was no way she could have killed him after dawn. She had no alibi for the middle of the night, though . . . the time it was now. But right now the mountains weren't visible. And if Miura couldn't see the mountains either, how did he draw that picture? It was impossible . . .

Or was it? Iwata began to doubt his reasoning. Maybe it would have been impossible for most people, but Miura had been an art teacher for nearly twenty years. He was an expert.

On top of that, he loved this view and had come here over and over again to draw it. Couldn't he have drawn it from memory on that night?

Even Iwata, poor artist that he was, felt confident he could roughly draw the outside of his own house from memory.

But even assuming Miura did draw the view from memory, why did he do it? Why, in his final moments, did he draw a view he could not see?

The voice came again.

'You're trying to destroy our happiness.'

'*Our?*'

'You're getting in the way of Haruto and me living our lives . . .'

Haruto . . . He remembered that name.

Miura's son. His only child.

174

'I have to kill you, don't you see?'

The woman's fingers suddenly touched his lips, then forced their way into his mouth.

'Come on . . . Eat . . . your dinner . . .'

Something flowed into his mouth. It was a thick, chunky liquid that tasted somehow familiar . . . It tasted of . . . Yes, of meatballs, vegetable tempura, rice. All mixed together. The contents of the Hanayagi Bento, blended into a paste.

She . . . She couldn't have . . .

He must not swallow. He tried to spit it out, but she pressed her hand to his mouth.

'Go on. Eat.'

It was undeniable now. She was killing him exactly the same way she had killed Miura.

'If you don't eat . . . you'll die . . .'

The woman used her other hand to pinch Iwata's nose. He couldn't breathe. He tried to shake her hands off his face, but she only pressed harder.

Iwata did all he could to avoid swallowing, but soon he grew desperate for air. After about a minute, he was at his limit. His head was pounding. The cells of his body were crying out for oxygen. The woman said, 'I'll let you breathe, if you just swallow.'

His brain said, 'No!' But his body would not listen. His throat swallowed as if of its own accord.

The liquid flowed down his throat and into his stomach.

The woman removed her hands. Iwata gasped for breath.

And then, once more, she pinched his nose and poured the fluid into his mouth.

This time, he swallowed. He had not given up, though.

For now, he would do as he was told. He would catch his breath, gather strength and wait for his chance to escape. He was a young man. He was stronger than his tormentor. He would have his chance.

But then, as if she had read Iwata's thoughts, the woman picked up the rock again. She drove it into Iwata's eye. With a spike of pain, his vision clouded and went red. He tried to blink. He felt blood leaking from his eye, down the side of his head.

It was all going wrong. He could not move. He could not see.

But Iwata refused to give up. He knew he would have a chance. He could turn it around. He still believed it. But at the same time, he had another thought.

If he died here, as a journalist, he had to leave something behind. Some information.

Inside his sleeping bag, he moved his hands, straining his wrists to the limit. He teased a pencil and receipt from his pocket and folded the paper.

Using his fingers to feel the position of the folds, he began to draw.

He did not know if he could do as well as Miura, but he had to draw.

To tell whoever found it who had killed him and Miura.

On September 21, 1995, the body of a man was discovered at the eighth station of Mt K— in L— Prefecture. The deceased was Shunsuke Iwata, a newspaper employee. A drawing of mountain scenery was left at the scene.

.　　.　　.

September 26, 1995.

The body of a man was discovered in his room in an apartment complex in Fukui Prefecture. The deceased was forty-three-year-old Nobuo Toyokawa. Tests revealed massive amounts of sleeping pills in Toyokawa's system. Police have ruled it a suicide.

A short letter, believed to be a suicide note, was found in the room.

I'm sorry.

I am the one who killed Yoshiharu Miura and Shunsuke Iwata.

I hope my death will serve as penance. Goodbye.

Nobuo Toyokawa

It had been typed on a word processor.

Naomi Konno stared down at the mysterious man collapsed in her hall.

The grey hood had been drawn back and the face that it revealed was familiar. The face of someone she had met once, long ago. But she could not recall where.

'Who are you?'

The man, pressing one hand to the stab wound in his side, struggled to speak. 'I guess . . . It's no wonder you don't remember. It's been over twenty years since we met. Since . . . Since I interviewed you . . .'

'Interviewed?'

'I . . . was a reporter . . . Name's Kumai. Been a while, Naomi Miura. Sorry. Right. . . . You're using your maiden name. Konno. . . . Took me . . . a while to find you.'

She dredged up the memory.

Kumai. A reporter. She'd met him only once, after the murder.

'Kumai? Why . . . What are you doing here?'

'While back . . . You paid a visit to a guy under me. Man name of Iwata. . . . Remember?'

An image rose suddenly in Naomi's mind.

A battered mass of flesh in the darkness.

'Naomi . . . Come on, you need to fess up. This is the time. Hey! Some backup, please!'

At those words, another man pushed through the doorway into the apartment.

'Naomi Konno!' he shouted. 'This is the police! You're under arrest for attempted murder!'

THE FINAL CHAPTER

The Bird, Safe in the Tree

Naomi Konno

Naomi sat in the cold detention cell and stared, blank-faced, at the wall.

It had been several days since that man . . . that Kumai . . . had come to her home and shattered her family's peace. A peace that had been threatened over and over again. There was always someone getting in the way.

Her life replayed in her mind's eye, flashes of events speeding by like a magic lantern.

The first memory was from her childhood.

. . .

Naomi knew that she was a child of a happy home.

She lived in one of Tokyo's best districts, and her father was a sincere, gentle man. He loved Naomi. Her mother, always standing by him with a kind smile on her face, was a beautiful woman with long, black, lustrous hair and pale skin.

On parents' day, she remembered feeling such pride to see her mother—so beautiful, so elegant—standing among the other mothers there, sunburnt, fat and wrinkled.

On Naomi's tenth birthday, her parents took her out for dinner. As she filled herself with a hamburger steak in the department store restaurant, her father said, 'Next, I think we'll go buy your present, Naomi. What would you like?'

Naomi thought it over. What should she ask for?

'Anything you want, darling. You've been studying so hard lately. As a treat. Even if it's a bit expensive. Go ahead, say the word,' he went on.

She knew if she didn't say something now, the chance might never come again. She decided to go for broke, all or nothing.

'I'd like a finch please, Father.'

A while ago, when she'd been out shopping with her mother, Naomi had seen a little finch in the window of the pet shop. Its sharp beak. Its little round body. Its sparkling eyes. She'd fallen in love in an instant. Since then, every day, she had dreamed of a life with the darling thing. She knew, though, that her mother did not like animals, so she had never revealed her wish.

'I see. A finch, is it? I wonder what Mother will say . . .' Father turned to Mother, a slight frown on his face. So, it was up to her. She only sighed, as if resigned, and said, 'Do what you like.' Her voice was empty. In her heart, Naomi was dancing for joy.

On their way home, the three stopped by the pet shop. The finch had grown a little larger, a little rounder.

'You have to take care of it yourself, now,' Father said, and Naomi nodded vigorously.

. . .

From that day on, life was just like her dreams.

She would come home from school and head straight to her room. There was the finch, sitting calmly in the cage her father had bought.

'Cheepy! I'm home!'

She had named the bird Cheepy, for the sounds he made.

At first, the bird had been wary of her, but Naomi had fed him every day, taken oh so gentle care of him, mimicked his cries and talked to him lovingly, so that now he had grown used to her. Now, when she opened his cage, he would fly straight to her hand. When she reached out, Cheepy would rub his head on her finger, as if wanting to be petted.

The sight of him eating so intently, preening so solemnly and carefully, curling up to sleep . . . So adorable, so beautiful, so full of love. It was the first time Naomi had ever felt such things.

With her father's help, she started her first ever woodworking project to build Cheepy a playhouse. After all their hard work, when they set out the dollhouse-like 'villa' they'd made and Cheepy scrambled inside, Naomi and her father clapped their hands in delight.

Mother just grimaced, and said, 'All that trouble for a bird?' But still, she looked on as her daughter and husband had their fun. What joy. Naomi had hoped those days would go on forever. She thought they would.

But then, tragedy struck.

One day, just over a year after Cheepy came to live with them, Father died.

He killed himself. He had suffered from depression, something that no one spoke about in Japan, especially in those days. With his promotion to management, his workplace had become

183

an increasing source of stress. For the six months before he took his life, he had been visiting a mental clinic.

Mother didn't cry. She simply sat, silent, before the family Buddhist altar. As Naomi grew older, she learned to understand that feeling. When faced with true sorrow, people lose even the strength to shed tears.

.   .   .

After Father died, Mother changed. Naomi saw it happen.

They had canned food every day for dinner. Her mother stopped cleaning and doing laundry, and soon the house was littered with rubbish. The cause of her father's death likely made everything worse. If he had died of an illness or in an accident, at least others might have shown some sympathy. They might have offered some words of comfort, and perhaps extended some kind of support.

As it was . . .

'I do wonder why that Konno killed himself . . .'

'I reckon because his wife was cheating on him, don't you?'

'She's certainly got the face for it.'

'Makes you wonder if the girl is even his, it does.'

Naomi could not help overhearing the rumours, utterly baseless as they were. Her mother withdrew, staying at home more and more, as if seeking to escape the suspicious eyes of her neighbours. Mother had never been on friendly terms with them anyway, so now there was no one to take her side.

Loneliness, grief, rage . . . Mother took out all her emotional pain on Naomi. And, as is the way of such things, she eventually turned to violence. But Naomi endured.

If I am a good girl and bear it, then mother will surely go back to normal one day.

She told herself that, over and over, as she stroked Cheepy with her bruised hands.

She started cleaning and doing the laundry unbidden, hoping to make Mother happy. She put a smile on her face, even in the bad times. She even tried to cook, although she could only manage simple things. One day, she thought she'd try whipping up her mother's favorite dish, chopped burdock root braised in soy sauce and sugar. She took her pocket money to buy the ingredients and spent two hours cooking it. In the end, it didn't look great but she thought it tasted nice.

She went to get a plate from the cupboard to take to her mother's room, but she was careless. The plate slipped from her hand and shattered on the floor. The sound drew her mother from her room.

She's going to hit me!

As if utterly unaware of Naomi, who stood bracing herself, Mother began cleaning up the shattered plate.

'Mother . . . I'm sorry. Um. I made . . . burdock . . .'

Naomi forced out the words, her voice quivering. Mother continued to pick up the shards as she muttered, as if to herself, 'It should have been you who died, not him.'

And that is when Naomi understood.

Her mother had not changed. She had always been like this. She had never loved Naomi. In fact, Naomi could not recall a single time when she and her mother had talked or played together, just the two of them. All of her happy family memories had been because of her father.

Her mother had been able to stand there, smiling gently,

185

because Father was next to her. She had merely played at being the caring mother for Father's sake, to ensure his love.

And at the same time, Naomi discovered something about herself. She had always been proud of her beautiful mother, but she had never felt anything else for her. Not once. They could be together as mother and child only with Father there uniting them. Now, with Father dead, they were simply two women.

The Konno family had never been as happy as Naomi had thought.

.   .   .

The incident was inevitable. It was the afternoon of the first of September, the first day back at school after the summer holidays.

Naomi came home after the school opening ceremony, opened the front door and heard a screeching cry. It was Cheepy. It was a terrible sound, unlike any she had ever heard before.

Filled with dread, she ran to her room. She opened the door. Mother stood there in the middle of the room. The birdcage lay at her feet. She held Cheepy clenched in her right hand. The bird struggled painfully in her grasp. Mother turned towards Naomi, a small smile on her face.

'Ah, Naomi. This bird has been screeching all day. It was making such a racket I couldn't sleep.'

'What . . . Why?'

Cheepy was a quiet thing. He had never made much noise before. *Why today?* Naomi thought furiously, then had her answer.

Naomi had been with Cheepy all through the summer holidays. They had played together from morning to night. He must have gotten lonely today, when his owner had gone back to school for the first time in so long. He must have been calling for Naomi. She found him so brave and sweet, it brought tears to her eyes.

'Mother . . . I'm sorry. It's all right now. He'll be quiet now. Please, let him go.'

'Hush. Like you can teach it anything.'

'That's not it. Cheepy was just lonely because I was gone.'

'That's not it?! Is that how you talk to your mother? Oh, the cheek!'

Naomi knew there was nothing she could say. She dropped to hands and knees, head bowed to the floor, begging.

'Mother, forgive me. It was all my fault. Please, hit me. Beat me all you want. I can bear it. Just, please, let Cheepy go,' she cried out, ready to sacrifice herself. Cheepy's voice grew quieter.

Oh, thank goodness. She's forgiven him.

She raised her eyes at the thought, but what she saw set her shivering. Mother's hand was squeezing more tightly, crushing Cheepy. He had no more energy to cry out, and his head lolled weakly.

'Mother! Please . . . Cheepy's going to die!'

'That's what I'm hoping!'

Naomi gasped.

The words sent her into a rage.

As if by pure reflex, she leapt at her mother. It was the first time she had ever fought back. But her mother struck out, kicking Naomi in the stomach and sending her flying.

She's going to kill him. What can I do?

Her gaze fell on something that sat in the corner of the room. It was Cheepy's wooden playhouse, the one she had built with

187

her father. Naomi ran over, picked it up and threw it in her mother's face.

Taken by surprise, her mother was knocked off balance and fell on her backside.

Naomi saw her chance. She took up the playhouse again and, using all her strength, brought it down on her mother's head. Her upper body collapsed, as if stunned.

Naomi tried to free Cheepy, but her mother's fist remained tightly clenched around the tiny body.

What can I do?!

After a moment, Mother sat up and glared at Naomi with hate in her eyes. As she did, Cheepy gave a low 'Screee' from her fist. It sounded like his last gasp before dying.

It was that noise that made up her mind.

Naomi stood and kicked her mother back to the ground, then she jumped with all her weight on her mother's belly, landing two-footed. With a sound like a massive belch, bloody foam erupted from Mother's mouth.

Naomi raised her left foot and stomped with all her weight on Mother's neck.

There was a barely audible crack. Mother's eyes rolled back in her head and her mouth gaped. Naomi had won.

Naomi frantically freed Cheepy. She gently grasped the tiny body, and he rubbed his head on her finger, as if seeking comfort.

'Oh, thank goodness. He's still alive.'

Her heart was filled to bursting with warmth and love.

Naomi sat next to her mother's corpse, weeping tears of joy.

. . .

Naomi spent the next six years in a juvenile reformatory. Cheepy was allowed to stay in the facility staffroom, and Naomi was left in charge of his care. This would not normally have been allowed. The special treatment came about because of a statement from the young woman counsellor who'd taken charge of Naomi's psychoanalysis.

'Naomi's drawing shows a tree protecting a small bird. That is an expression of maternal love seated deep in her heart . . . [and] her desire to protect creatures weaker than herself. At the same time, the large, sharp thorns would seem to indicate a prickly, aggressive nature. However, if we bring her into contact with animals and children, it should help soften that element.'

Life at the facility was strict and highly controlled, but it was far more pleasant than living alone with Mother. Above all, Naomi was happy and grateful that she could be with Cheepy.

In the autumn of her sixth year there, Cheepy passed quietly away, under Naomi's loving eyes.

Thank you. You gave me the strength to go on.

She buried Cheepy in a secluded corner of the facility grounds. Six months later, Naomi graduated high school and left the facility.

After that, she rented a cheap apartment in the city and began attending nursing school to become a midwife. The inspiration had been a somewhat offhand comment from a staff member at her reformatory, along the lines of, 'Naomi, your maternal instincts are so strong. I can see you in a caring profession. I bet you'd make a great midwife.'

There was more than a little irony in the idea that a girl who had murdered her own mother might become a midwife, but she also felt that with her unusual educational background, she had little chance at finding employment at a larger company. And in Japan in those days, there were few opportunities for women to get professional qualifications. So, reluctantly, she chose midwifery.

She had a mountain of work to get through every day at nursing school. She had never minded studying, so it was no real burden, but she did struggle financially.

Her student loans were not enough to live on, so she started to work part-time at a cafe three days a week. The cafe was on the way to a nearby art school, so most of the regular clientele were art students. One of them was named Yoshiharu Miura.

His plain looks, along with his short undyed hair and his daily uniform of jeans and white T-shirt, actually made him stand out amid the more flamboyantly dressed art students. Their relationship, born out of casual small talk, deepened eventually

190

to the point that they would discuss their personal lives and worries.

He introduced her to new friends. One, Nobuo Toyokawa, was a young man attending art school with Miura. Miura always talked about Toyokawa as a born artist. That was no exaggeration, as Naomi saw it, because the pictures Toyokawa produced were in a different league.

Eventually, Miura and Toyokawa started coming to Naomi's apartment to hang out. With Naomi busy studying, they took to bringing over dinner and cleaning her apartment for her. Even as she enjoyed her time with them, Naomi started to understand something.

The two boys are competing over me . . . This was no mere vanity. Every time she looked in the mirror, her certainty grew.

I have my mother's beauty. Pale skin. Long, dark, silky hair. She was the spitting image of her mother.

.   .   .

Things came to a head one summer afternoon. As he and Naomi were sitting together in her stuffy room, Miura said, 'Next year, after I graduate, I'm going back to my hometown to become an art teacher. Would you come with me, Naomi?'

It was a characteristically awkward proposal. Naomi said yes on the spot. Toyokawa truly was a charming man, but Naomi loved Miura's straightforward character.

She had decided to remain quiet about her past.

The following spring, Miura and Naomi both graduated from their respective schools. They were so busy with job hunting and moving at the same time that their wedding ceremony came a year later, after they had moved to L— Prefecture. Toyokawa dropped everything and made the journey out to attend. Despite the awkwardness, he congratulated them with a smile on his face.

Life after marriage was difficult but fulfilling. Miura got a job teaching at a local high school, and Naomi became a midwife at a small maternity hospital. Although she had only chosen the profession because of an offhand remark, once she actually started doing it, she came to see it as her life's calling.

Giving birth is not some beautiful sacred rite, as so many men seem to imagine. It is hours of tears and screaming, enduring pain and suffering with death always near, all to force a baby from your body. . . . In a word, it is torture. But to Naomi's eye, the faces of mothers after getting through it were beautiful. She devoted herself to those women: helping, comforting and encouraging them, even scolding them when necessary.

A few years later, Naomi became pregnant herself, but wrestled for a long time with the question of whether she should keep the child. Her greatest worry was her own mother. Even after she died, she had never left Naomi alone. When she looked in the mirror, her mother stared back at her.

I look like Mother. If I have a baby, won't I act like she did, too? Won't I beat my child, never feeling an ounce of love?

The thought terrified her.

But at the same time, there was an opposing desire: to have her child, raise it right and prove herself better than her mother.

She wanted to puff out her chest and say, 'I am not like you.' In the end, she decided to have her baby. Naomi's motherhood began out of a desire for revenge.

When the day came, her delivery was more difficult than she had anticipated. Near to fainting from the pain, Naomi forgot

192

herself in the struggle. When she finally held her baby on the delivery table, an almost-forgotten feeling began to fill her bleary mind. Joy, welling up from the very depths of her heart, as she had felt only once before in her life. The happiness of watching over a precious life. Infinite love . . . Ah, yes. That feeling.

The same feeling she'd had when holding Cheepy next to her mother's corpse.

A chill ran through her. She felt the wheels of her dark fate turning.

. . .

They named their son Haruto. Her husband had thought of it.

The anxiety she'd felt when she first got pregnant . . . the fear that she might not love her own child, just as her mother had failed to love her, disappeared as soon as her son was born. Naomi found him so darling it was almost unbearable. She poured all the love she had into her son, this weak, fragile, unsteady creature, who could not survive without her. Haruto had finally freed Naomi from her mother's curse.

As he grew, however, she saw that Haruto was different from other children. When she commented that he was withdrawn, many of the mothers of older children would laugh and say, 'Our little one was the same way at that age.' But Haruto took it further. He simply did not communicate with anyone other than Naomi.

When he went to primary school, the problem worsened. While his classmates all made friends and ran outside to play as soon as classes ended, Haruto always came home alone and shut himself in his room to read.

Her husband did not care for this and took to scolding his son.

'Haruto! A boy is supposed to go outside, run around, get strong!'

'Don't shut yourself indoors all day. Go and make lots of friends!'

'When you run into the neighbours outside, speak up and say hello! It's shameful, the way you just stand there and fidget!'

Naomi took the opposite approach to raising their son. If Haruto didn't want to go out, he could stay in the house. If he didn't want to talk to people, there was no need to make him. Trying to force him to act in ways he didn't want would only traumatize the boy and make him withdraw even more. Her insistence on that put the two at odds, and the couple's relationship slowly deteriorated.

One day, as Naomi stood in the kitchen cooking, Haruto ran in and clung to her, a terrified look on his face. Something was clearly wrong.

'What happened? Tell Mummy . . .' she said. Haruto did, his voice on the verge of tears.

'Papa hit me.'

Naomi immediately went to confront him.

'I told Haruto to go outside and play,' he answered, 'and that boy just turned and stuck out his tongue at me. Showing that kind of attitude to a parent? It's unacceptable. If we don't teach him the proper way to behave now, it'll go poorly for him in the future.'

'But . . . You hit him for that?'

'Spare the rod, spoil the child. The way I see it, when a child passes the age of ten, their ego starts to rear up. If all you do is talk to them, they won't listen at all. From now on, he'll get the physical discipline he needs. It's a parent's duty.'

She couldn't believe her ears. You should start hitting children after the age of ten? She'd never heard such a thing.

Her husband had always been stubborn, unyielding in his view of the world. When Naomi was younger, she'd found his forthrightness attractive. She now cursed her past self for thinking that way. Having to live with such a person in her family was hell.

From then on, he started regularly hitting Haruto. Naomi argued with him, but he would never listen.

And that was not the end of it. On their days off, he would drag the miserable boy out camping and force him to eat piles of grilled meat, which he hated. The boy was afraid of insects but had to sleep outdoors. And if Haruto protested, his father would slap him, saying, 'You've no manners!'

She knew he wasn't doing it out of malice. It was, in his own way, an expression of love. He truly did think it was his duty as a father. And that just made everything so much more difficult.

Through the next couple of years, she pitied Haruto deeply. She knew all too well the terror of living under the same roof as a violent parent. She soon began to contemplate divorce in earnest, thinking it was the only way to protect Haruto. But one thing worried her.

In a divorce, custody almost always went to the mother, without a very compelling reason otherwise. Naomi, though, had a past she could not erase.

Her husband did not know. She had told him her mother died of illness. But it would not take long for someone to find out if they started digging. And if that happened, the court would surely find her an unfit mother. There was a risk that her husband would be given sole custody of Haruto.

And without me, Haruto will be . . .

The thought of what might happen gave her chills.

And then, suddenly, a long-forgotten feeling came back to her.

A feeling like that day when she was a child, the afternoon after the first day of class, when she saw her mother crushing Cheepy. The vision of Cheepy crying out in her fist melted into one of Haruto now. Naomi's mind was made up.

She would kill her husband.

.   .   .

'I'm going hiking up Mt K— tomorrow. I'm camping at the eighth station. Could you pack my things?'

It was the evening of September 19, 1992. When she heard her husband's words, Naomi put together her plan.

Isamu Kumai

May 8, 2015. A hospital in Tokyo

'It's closed up pretty well. It doesn't look like there's any infection, so I think you'll be able to go home sometime next week,' the nurse fastening his bandages said in a nasal voice. 'Oh, one more thing, Mr Kumai. A new patient is moving into the bed next to yours. You be sure to get along! Now, then . . .'

With that, she turned and trotted out of his hospital room as light as a dancer.

Be sure to get along? What am I, a pre-schooler?

Kumai stared up at the unchanging white ceiling. He was tired of the sight. He had been in this room for two weeks, and if he turned on his side, his wound wouldn't heal properly. But he was alive. That was a confusing feeling.

That evening, two weeks before, when he had rung Naomi Konno's doorbell, he had been prepared to die. And the truth was, if that first stab had gone higher and hit his heart, he most certainly would have. But, in the end, Kumai had survived.

He closed his eyes and played back the events for the umpteenth time.

The first image that arose was from Shunsuke Iwata's funeral. His grandfather's face. Haggard, devoid of all hope. The face of a man who had survived his grandchild.

It's my fault your grandson died.

If only I'd never talked about that murder.

If only I'd never mentioned going back to his high school.

The words had risen in his throat but failed to come out. He hated his own cowardice.

.   .   .

The circumstances of Iwata's death were identical to those of Yoshiharu Miura's. The police investigated it as a second murder by the same perpetrator. And then, their prime suspect in the Miura murder, Nobuo Toyokawa, committed suicide and left a note written on a word processor, confessing to both crimes. With the murderer dead, the case was closed.

This was how the police decided it had happened:

September 1995. Iwata visited his old school, met Yuki Kameido and asked for Nobuo Toyokawa's new address. Since she didn't have it, the following day she visited Naomi Konno, who had also known Toyokawa, to ask for the address. But Konno did not know it, either. She did know his phone number, though, so she called him to ask. And when she did, she told him, 'A

197

man named Iwata is looking into that old case. And tomorrow, the anniversary of Yoshiharu's death, he's planning to climb Mt K— in memory of my husband.' When Toyokawa heard that, he grew afraid that his past crime would be discovered, so he decided to kill Iwata. The day of the memorial hike, he killed Iwata in the same place as Miura, using the same method. But then he found himself unable to live with the guilt and took his own life.

It did, indeed, seem reasonable. Kumai himself had thought that Toyokawa was the murderer. But one thing didn't sit right.

Why had Toyokawa written the note on that word processor?

The police said they had found a brand-new one in Toyokawa's house. It seemed that he had gone out to buy it just to write his suicide note. Wasn't that odd? All he had needed was a pen and paper. Why go to all that trouble?

Kumai thought about it. Perhaps the murderer was someone else. The real murderer had taken the word processor to Toyokawa's house, killed him in a way that looked like suicide, and used it to write the fake note to disguise their handwriting.

Naturally, the police had thought of that as well. But in the end, they decided Toyokawa had indeed committed suicide. It was easy to see why they had stopped investigating at that point.

Toyokawa had died in Fukui Prefecture. It was quite far from L— Prefecture, where Miura and Iwata had been killed. In a case like that, the police of the two prefectures had to coordinate, which sometimes made the investigation on both sides far sloppier.

Anyway, Kumai wasn't convinced. He thought they should look even deeper into the murder. Iwata's spirit could not rest until the truth was revealed.

If the police won't do it, then I'll chase down the truth for them.

Kumai started researching the cases in his free time while still working for the paper. The main reason was to assuage his guilt as Iwata's boss. But another feeling drove him, as well.

Kumai could not forget something Iwata had said before his death.

'I won't cause any trouble for the paper. I really just want to follow up on Mr Miura's case as a personal thing, outside of work.' He had found it admirable. Kumai had been rotting since his transfer from editorial. Iwata, though, was still determined to work on this story, even after getting a post he never wanted. Who had been more deserving of the title 'journalist'? The answer was obvious.

Kumai wanted his pride back. He couldn't let the boy beat him.

.   .   .

In the end, the most important clue for Kumai's private investigation was the picture Iwata left behind.

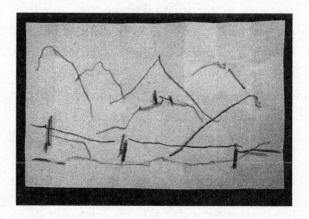

Iwata drew the mountain scenery on the back of a receipt that had been in his pocket. It was the view from the eighth station. He had made folds in the paper.

In other words, he had mimicked Miura's actions. But why? What had Iwata been trying to show with this picture?

"Mr Kumai! Here's your new neighbour!'

The nasal voice pulled him back to reality.

The nurse came into the room pushing a wheelchair. His 'new neighbour' was a young man with a cast on his leg. The young man stared intently into Kumai's eyes and said, 'Pardon me for intruding.'

'No problem. Welcome,' Kumai answered and went back to his musing.

.   .   .

Iwata . . . If you'd been put in the editorial department like you'd wanted, you'd have made one hell of a reporter.

It had taken Kumai ten years to arrive at the same truth Iwata had found in only two weeks. The trick of faking the time of death, the reason for the stolen sleeping bag and food, and for the horribly mutilated body . . . When he realized what it all meant, Kumai grew convinced that Yuki Kameido was the real murderer.

If the crime had occurred after dawn on the 21st, both Toyokawa and Naomi were in the clear. The only one of the three suspects who didn't have an alibi for the time in question was Kameido. He thought he had solved it. But no one would listen. In the end, Kumai's theory was nothing more than a guess, and a civilian's guess was not enough to get the police to reopen a closed investigation. Especially one ten years old. For police headquarters, it was ancient history.

Kumai still refused to give up.

I just need to find proof. Then the police will have to get moving.

But that thought is what led him into the labyrinth.

No matter how deep he dug into Kameido, he couldn't find a single lead connecting her to the murder.

What kind of tricks could a young girl like that use to erase every trace of a murder?

Despite his impatience, he made no progress. Just wasted more time.

A turning point came, but only years later. He found the lead that solved it all in the most unexpected place.

One evening, Kumai was watching television at home. He was flipping mindlessly through the channels when he happened across a documentary about an artist. The artist told the camera:

'It was when I was a kid. I used to practise drawing from memory. For example, let's say you have a photograph. A picture of a cat, say. I'd stare at it for ten seconds and I'd memorize the shape of that cat. After ten seconds, I'd turn the picture over, and try to draw a picture of the cat on my sketchpad. I did that over and over, and I think now it's one of my biggest assets. I can perfectly recreate any scene, no matter how complicated, after seeing it once.'

Drawing from memory. He'd never even thought of it. Kumai knew nothing of art and had never drawn a picture, even for fun. It was simply a given for him that you couldn't draw a picture of something without looking at the real thing.

Kumai decided to try it himself. He got a pen and memo pad and tried to sketch the view from the eighth station on Mt

201

K— from memory. He surprised himself by more or less succeeding. It was a shock, but when he thought about it, it was obvious.

As he had chased down the truth, Kumai had looked at the pictures Miura and Iwata left almost every day for ten years. He hadn't been trying to memorize them, but they'd imprinted themselves on his brain without his realizing it. The human brain was a fascinating thing.

So, what about Miura and Iwata?

Before his death, Miura had drawn that scenery every time he visited the eighth station.

Iwata had looked at his picture every day, trying to discover its meaning.

So, wouldn't both of them have been able to draw those mountains without needing to see the real things? If that was the case, if they could have drawn the mountains even in the dark of the night, then they might not have been murdered after dawn. And if so, there was one more suspect without an alibi for the time of the murder. Miura's wife, Naomi.

And if Naomi was the murderer, that would answer one more question that had been bothering him.

A basic question: why had the murderer left that picture at the scene?

If a victim drew a strange picture at the moment of their death, their murderer would surely think to destroy it or take it away. You wouldn't expect the kind of person who could plan such a complicated murder, including faking the time of death, to make a mistake like overlooking a dying message.

And to make the same mistake twice? The inexplicability of it had gnawed at his brain. But now he understood. It was no mistake.

The murderer had intentionally left the picture at the scene. They . . . No, *she* had understood that these pictures of the mountains worked in her favour.

Miura's drawing

Even if by chance the police saw through the staged time of death, the picture of the mountains, if the police took it to be a dying message from the victim, would lead them to revise their estimated time of death to after dawn. If so, anyone with an alibi for the morning would be cleared of suspicion.

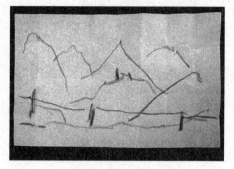

Iwata's drawing

Iwata must have drawn his own picture because he knew the murderer would leave it behind.

The murderer left the mountain scenery pictures behind, so that meant the murderer was someone who would benefit from them. That was Iwata's true dying message.

· · ·

After that realization, Kumai began to focus his efforts on Naomi. As he learned more about her, he was filled with regret over not investigating her from the start.

He found out that she had killed her mother as a child and spent six years in a juvenile reformatory. Kumai went to talk to the counsellor who had been in charge of her analysis at the time. Her name was Tomiko Hagio. Now, as an older woman, she was a famous psychologist who toured the country giving lectures.

Hagio spoke with some nostalgia.

'Ah, little Naomi. When she was a girl, she was the first case I was assigned. Poor little thing. Her mother abused her. It seems she came to depend on her pet bird for comfort from that pain. And then, one day, her mother was going to kill the bird. Naomi was desperate to protect it. That child had a powerful urge to protect, and I suppose it made her want to defend those weaker than herself.'

Hearing the story completed the picture.

'We were not a particularly close couple. We fought over parenting styles. . . . Well, for example, our son likes to stay in and read, but my husband kept dragging him out and making him go camping or have cookouts together. . . . Our son hated it. He would just do what he wanted, with no regard for our son, and he was so self-satisfied. All "I'm a good dad, devoted to my family".'

He was sure of it. The child was the motive.

Miura had become a violent man, and she had killed him to protect her child.

There was still one thing he didn't understand.

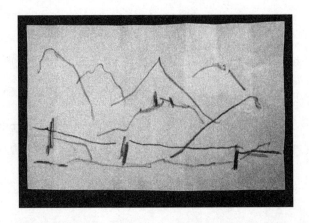

Why had Miura drawn that picture before his death? The picture had tricked Kumai into suspecting Kameido at first. It had kept him from discovering the truth for so long.

Miura had essentially covered for his wife. Why?

Naomi Konno

As he died, her husband had tried to say something. But before the words could form, she had crushed his windpipe with a stone. She had been desperate.

When it was all over, before she left the mountain, Naomi had searched the body and found the drawing in his pocket. Her thoughts raced, and she quickly decided that she should leave it behind.

Then, she had hiked down by the light of a pocket torch and returned home undiscovered. She had washed away all the traces on her body and set about her morning routine as if nothing had happened.

But that was not the end of it. In fact, it was only the lead-up to the main event. She would have to keep up her lie to the police and the press. She would have to play the part of a woman mourning the loss of her husband. She could not afford any mistakes.

If she were arrested, Haruto would lose his only parent. He would be alone. She could not let that happen. Even if it meant she was destined for hell after she died, to be devoured by demons for all eternity, she didn't care. All that mattered was that she had to protect Haruto.

·　　·　　·

She had no confidence in her performance. But she made no mistakes. She remained free, even six months after the murder.

As the media buzz around the case calmed, and she was no longer the target of repeated and repetitive interviews, Naomi's life finally began to settle down. And that is when her husband's drawing returned to her.

Looking back with a cooler head, she decided she had been right to leave the drawing at the scene. Even if, somehow, the police saw through her tricks, that picture would be her last refuge and keep her safe.

Wonderful. Haruto would not end up alone. The thought relieved her.

And she decided her husband must have thought the same thing.

He must have grasped Naomi's plan while she was force-feeding him the bento. Grasped that he was about to die. That there was no escape. And with him dead, if his wife was sentenced to death for his murder, there would be no one left to look after Haruto. So, he had desperately drawn that picture. Not to protect Naomi. To protect Haruto's mother. Or so Naomi imagined.

Tears filled her eyes. She couldn't say he had been a good father, but his love for his son had been real.

.   .   .

After her husband's death, the house grew livelier than ever.

Toyokawa and one of her husband's former students, a girl named Yuki Kameido, started coming over regularly out of concern for the two left behind. Toyokawa would bring things to eat, while Kameido helped with cooking and looking after Haruto. It

206

seemed that the boy, who had until now never confided in anyone besides his mother, could open up completely to Yuki.

Just as Naomi began to feel that this arrangement was not a bad substitute of family, things took a terrible turn.

One evening, after the four of them had enjoyed a hotpot meal, Yuki and Haruto went out to a nearby shop for some sweets. Naomi and Toyokawa were left behind, and suddenly he reached out to take her hand.

'Mr Toyokawa! Wh-what . . . ?!'

'Naomi . . . Would you like to hear something interesting?' Toyokawa whispered in her ear, a leer on his face. 'That night? I was there. At the eighth station.'

She froze.

Naomi tried to appear cool as she slapped Toyokawa's hand away. 'Don't make such jokes. It's indecent!'

'Indecent, you say? Rich, coming from someone who killed her own husband.' Toyokawa groped her breasts with both hands. He squeezed like he was trying to pull them off.

'Stop! The children will be home soon!'

'Right, which is why we need to settle some things before they do.'

'What are you talking about?'

'Don't play stupid. That day, I was planning to kill Miura myself, you know.'

'What?'

'I hated the bastard. Not a drop of artistic talent in his body but acting like mister big shot just because he was a lousy art teacher. And treating me like some kind of assistant? I couldn't take it any more. I wanted him dead. That day, after we split up at the fourth station, I went off the trail and climbed up to the

207

eighth. I was planning on going after him when it got late and he was asleep. But then . . . Then, someone with the same idea beat me to it. Right, Miss Murderer? What did it feel like? Forcing that food down his throat, then slaughtering him?'

She didn't think he was bluffing, then. 'Forcing food down his throat . . .' If Toyokawa knew that, then he must have been there. He had witnessed it with his own eyes.

'Mr Toyokawa . . . Please . . . Don't tell the police.'

'Oh, no, I won't say a word. I'll need something from you in return, though. Let's make a deal. From now on. Every week. You give me what you know I want."

'No! I won't do it!'

'Then I go to the police!'

'You can't.'

'Give up, bitch. I know how you put me and Miura on the scales back in college, playing with us like toys. Then you tossed me away when Miura proposed. I've not forgotten. I've dreamed of shattering your happy little family all these years. It's what kept me alive all this time!'

Naomi thought furiously, wondering if she could kill this man, too.

But the timing was all wrong. If someone connected to the case died so soon after her husband, Naomi would become the prime suspect. She wouldn't get away with it again.

As bitter as it was, she accepted his deal. Toyokawa came to have his way with her every Saturday night. It was disgusting; his touch was obscene and selfish. Haruto was safe, at least. She told herself that all she had to do was endure it.

But one night disaster struck.

Haruto woke up for the toilet and caught them in the act. It was only a moment, but he saw. Naomi panicked and slammed the sliding door shut.

'Oh dear, the boy's only gone and seen it all!' Toyokawa said with a nasty grin. It made her immediately suspicious. She was certain she'd shut the sliding door before they started. She did it every time, just in case Haruto did wake up.

What's more, Haruto had always been a deep sleeper who hardly ever woke during the night. He got up for the toilet maybe a couple of times a year. Why today, of all days?

She found out why the next morning. She discovered a small box labelled 'Torsemide' in the kitchen bin. It was a medicine she'd encountered often in her medical training. A diuretic.

With a chill, she recalled Toyokawa's grin the night before.

He'd wanted Haruto to see. Wanted to show him his mother's disgrace.

Naomi could feel herself filling with dark, murderous rage.

The only thing that kept her from acting on it was that Toyokawa was transferred soon afterwards. With the filthy man far from her home, Naomi could finally start living a more human life.

But, as Naomi's fate seemed to dictate, danger came again.

.   .   .

It was in September 1995, three years after the murder. Yuki Kameido came to visit the house. After graduating from high school, she'd gone on to study art at L— Prefecture University, and she'd been so busy with her work that her visits had grown infrequent. They shared a meal, then Yuki mentioned something unexpected.

'By the way, do you happen to know where Mr Toyokawa is living these days?'

'Why?'

'A little while back someone from the newspaper, a Mr Iwata, came to talk to me. He says he's looking into your husband's murder. Can you believe it?'

Naomi broke out in a cold sweat. It had been three years since the murder. The investigation was all but closed. Why now?

'Does this Mr Iwata have any connection with my husband?'

'He was a student of his, he says.'

Which meant that this was not pure journalistic interest, but something personal. Something much more dangerous.

'Yuki . . . Could you tell me more?'

Isamu Kumai

Kumai lay in bed thinking back to his own mother.

In contrast to his slender father, she had been as big around as a barrel, always enjoying a drink and a laugh. She'd been a cheerful woman, but when she was angry at her son, she would take on the face of a devil and call down the thunder and lighting. Kumai had feared his mother more than anyone in the world and trusted her more too.

One summer day, Kumai had been beaten up by the local bully. He came home with a lump on his head. Mum had cornered him and demanded, 'Who did that to you?' He had coughed up the bully's name, and been pulled along to the boy's house.

The boy's father was a brute of a man with a scarred face. He had a frightening air about him, and everyone suspected he had 'connections'. But Kumai's mother was unfazed.

She looked up at the towering brute and bombarded him with complaints, on the verge of grabbing the man by his collar. Kumai could recall her face as she did it as clear as day. She had lost her mind.

If the man's wife hadn't intervened, his mother might have killed him. Kumai, as young as he was, felt certain of it.

So, what made his own mother and Naomi different?

If his mother had made one wrong move, she might have turned out the same.

The thought, as chilling as it was, was not one Kumai could deny.

Naomi Konno

She had fretted to the very end over whether Iwata and Toyokawa needed killing. She knew she would be suspected if they both died. She shouldn't take that risk lightly.

But then, leaving Toyokawa alive was a risk in itself. The man had witnessed her commit murder. He was keeping quiet, but he could change his mind and go to the police at any time. And more than anything, Toyokawa had hated her and her husband. Naturally, he couldn't think much better of their son, little Haruto. If he ever put Haruto in danger . . .

It really would be best to kill them. First Iwata, then Toyokawa, and lay all the blame on him.

·   ·   ·

Once it was done, Naomi moved with Haruto to Tokyo, as if trying to escape her deeds. They rented a cheap sixth-floor apartment, and she took a job at a nearby maternity clinic.

211

Despite the anxiety eating away at her, the days and months passed in tranquillity.

Before she knew it, Naomi was nearing her sixtieth birthday. Haruto finished high school and found a job at a nearby ironworks. When he first started, he struggled to get used to the work, but by his third year or so, he had matured into a fully fledged working man. Naomi woke early every day to fix his lunchbox and help him get his working day off to a good start.

One day, Haruto came to Naomi with an uncomfortable look on his face, and said:

'Um. Mother. I've met someone I like. May I date her?'

Once Naomi recovered from her shock, she burst into laughter. She had always joked with him about making sure to inform his mother before he started dating anyone, but she had never dreamed he'd actually do it. Even as a grown man, Haruto still did as Mother said. Naomi patted his head and told him:

'Of course you may. But let me judge if she's fit for you first. Bring her home to meet me, all right?'

.   .   .

A week later, Haruto did as she'd told him and brought his girlfriend home. When Naomi saw her face, her knees almost gave out in shock.

'Y-Yuki?'

The girl Haruto had taken a fancy to was Yuki Kameido. Her husband's former student, the one who had come to visit all those times when they had lived in L— Prefecture. She seemed almost embarrassed as she said:

'It's good to see you again, Naomi. I hope you'll allow Haruto and me to date . . .'

Then, as they ate the dinner Naomi had cooked, Haruto and Yuki explained how they had come to reunite.

About a month before, a young man had come to work part-time at Haruto's ironworks. One day, chatting during their break, he mentioned a beautiful girl named Yuki Kameido he'd worked with at a nearby convenience store. Half thinking the name must be pure coincidence, Haruto went to investigate, unable to contain his curiosity.

He found her there at the convenience store, busy working the register, and was astounded. There was no mistake, it was the same old Yuki who used to come and play with him at home back in L— Prefecture. He waited outside until her shift ended and she stepped out. When he called out to her, Yuki came up short, her eyes wide with shock. It was twelve years since they had last seen each other. Yuki was now thirty-three and Haruto twenty-seven.

That evening, over dinner, the two talked of their lives since they had last met.

After Yuki finished art school, she had taken a job as a designer at a local company. But after five years there, the company announced layoffs and she was let go. She looked for work locally for a while, but nothing came of it. The longer she went without a job, the worse her already strained relationship with her parents got.

One day, they had an argument from which there was no coming back. She wrote them a letter breaking off all contact and left home.

With nowhere to go, Yuki had come to Tokyo in search of work. For the next few years, she had done freelance design and illustration work, but never managed to get her career off the ground. Now, she was living check to check through part-time work at the convenience store.

When Haruto learned how this girl he had idolized in his youth was suffering, he was shocked. He could not bear it. He offered her 10,000 yen on the spot to help with her bills, but she refused to accept it.

'I can't take your money. That would be too embarrassing.'

'Sorry . . . But I want to help.'

'Well then, you can buy me dinner sometime.'

From there, they met up again and again. Each time, they ate fast food and then went to a nearby park, where they sat on the benches and shared a can of juice as they talked for hours. It seemed a poor kind of dating for two grown adults, but for the two of them, it was great fun.

'Will you be my girlfriend?'

Haruto was the one who pushed for the next step. And Yuki said yes on the spot.

. . .

Naomi listened to the pair with conflicted feelings.

She had always thought of Yuki and Haruto as something like siblings with an age gap. The idea of them as romantic partners felt somehow wrong.

But if the two had feelings for each other, there was nothing she could say. And she was well aware what a lovely girl Yuki was. Naomi would much rather he date her than some stranger from who knew where. She decided to support them wholeheartedly.

A year later, they got engaged.

Yuki would leave her own apartment and move in with Haruto and Naomi.

Now and then, Naomi did feel wistful remembering the time before her son got married, but her happiness at gaining a daughter-in-law outweighed her sadness.

They all agreed there was no need to invite anyone from outside the city to a big ceremony, so they celebrated a quiet wedding at home. When they had cleaned up after dinner and Haruto had fallen asleep drunk, Naomi and Yuki sat in the kitchen, chatting about nothing in particular.

Until Yuki went quiet. Her expression grew grave, and she said, 'Naomi. There's something I've been hiding.'

'What? What's come over you all of a sudden?'

'I . . . was in love with Mr Miura.'

'. . . My late husband?'

'Yes. It started in my first year at school. I wore my hair short, but when he mentioned his wife wore hers long, I grew mine out. I did this,' she stroked her long hair, 'in imitation of you. When I ran into Haruto last year, it was such a shock. It was like Mr Miura had come back to life . . .'

'I suppose . . . He does have his father's looks. These last few years, especially.'

'Oh, but don't get me wrong! I'm not in love with Haruto as some kind of stand-in for his father. I love Haruto for himself. I just thought, if we're going to be living together, I shouldn't keep it hidden. I'm sorry. Maybe I've said too much.'

Naomi had no idea how to respond.

·   ·   ·

Even after that, their life together ran smoothly.

Yuki took over the housework as a full-time homemaker and did it impeccably. That freed up Naomi and Haruto to relax after returning home from work.

One morning, while Naomi was getting ready to leave for work, Yuki came out of her room, her face pale as a sheet.

'Naomi, I'm sorry. I'm not feeling well. I'm afraid I can't take care of things today.'

Yuki's condition sparked Naomi's professional instincts.

'Yuki, have you had your period recently?'

Naomi escorted her to the maternity clinic where she worked, and a test confirmed that Yuki was one month pregnant.

That evening, when Haruto came home from work and heard the news, he literally jumped for joy. He grabbed Yuki and thanked her, over and over. Yuki had been nervous the whole day, but, seeing his reaction, finally allowed herself to feel happy.

·   ·   ·

Naomi was happy for them. Or, she should have been.

But as Yuki's belly began to swell, so too did some vague feeling begin to well up in the depths of Naomi's heart. A sensation she could not identify. But it was something that made her uneasy, that much was certain.

One night, Naomi had a dream.

She held an infant to her breast. Looking to the side, she saw Haruto.

'Haruto, where's Yuki?'

'Yuki? Who's that?'

216

'Don't be silly. Yuki is this baby's mother.'

'Hahaha, what are you talking about? That baby's mother is . . .'

And Haruto pointed his finger at Naomi.

Even when she woke, the scene replayed itself over and over in her head.

Naomi understood. She wanted to be a mother again. She wanted to become that baby's mother, in a world without Yuki.

It was a dreadful desire.

But the dream had felt so, so sweet.

.   .   .

Naomi had taken charge of Yuki's prenatal check-ups from the start. Normally, that kind of special treatment wouldn't be allowed simply because she was the woman's mother-in-law.

But this clinic wasn't a normal one. There was only one doctor on staff—the head—and he had inherited it from his father, so he really had no idea how other clinics worked. He passed the majority of his work on to the midwives and spent most of the day wandering around the clinic with a big grin on his face. The result was that the midwives held all the power. At first, Naomi had struggled to get along with her overbearing co-workers, but as she kept working, putting up with all their haughty attitudes, at some point she became the most senior midwife in the clinic.

And now, there was no one left who could say no to her.

From the beginning, Naomi saw two major risk factors in Yuki's pregnancy.

The first was her age. Yuki was over thirty-five years old, which put her in the advanced maternal age range. The other was blood pressure. Yuki's was high. When she was nervous, in particular, her numbers often spiked far beyond the acceptable range, if only briefly.

Every time she saw those numbers, Naomi felt the darkness in her heart writhing.

. . .

Then came the 10th of September 2009. Yuki's contractions began at around ten in the morning.

She was admitted to the delivery room at around six in the evening. Things had gone smoothly up to that point.

Even after a few hours of pushing, however, the baby would not come. Then, suddenly, Yuki lost consciousness on the table. The clinic was thrown into a panic. One of the other midwives cried out, 'Hold on! Why is her blood pressure so high?!'

. . .

Two months before her due date, during Yuki's seventh month of pregnancy, Naomi's darkness had swollen to the point of bursting.

I am going to become a grandmother. I will be a withered old thing, always smiling, always gentle, spoiling my grandchild. Is that enough?

There was only one answer.

No. Absolutely not. I am . . . I am a mother.

It was like a dam had burst within her heart.

The next morning, Naomi handed Yuki three capsules to swallow.

'Yuki, Haruto tells me you've been feeling a little anemic lately, right? It's common in pregnancy, don't you worry. Pregnant women have trouble getting enough nutrients in general, not just iron, so you should take some supplements. I took these every day during my pregnancy. They helped a lot.'

The capsules contained only salt.

But Yuki trusted Naomi, so she took them without a second thought. People with high blood pressure are recommended to limit salt intake to no more than six grams a day. Every day, Yuki was taking fifteen grams of salt in her capsules.

It was like a kind of prayer.

The chances of success were slim. It was mostly a way to ease her mind. If it didn't work, then she would quit. She would support the two young people from the shadows. She would be an old woman, withering away. That might indeed be a greater happiness for Naomi.

But . . . The prayer was answered.

.   .   .

An emergency caesarean saw the baby delivered safely. The mother could not be saved.

Yuki had burst a blood vessel in her brain after hours of bearing down and pushing under a spike of extremely high blood pressure. No one at the hospital questioned it. Her pre-delivery medical chart showed her blood pressure as normal.

Of course it did. Naomi had been in charge of her testing and had falsified the numbers.

The next day, Naomi tendered her resignation.

She felt that she no longer had the right to call herself a midwife.

. . .

The unbearably sweet dream had become reality. Naomi had become a mother to a newborn infant, Yuta.

'Haruto, this child lost his mother at birth, right? I worry that when he gets older and starts to make friends, he'll feel sad to be the only one without a mother. I know it might be hard for you, but I think I should be his mama. I know I'm an old woman, but it's better than not having anyone, isn't it?'

It had been easy to convince Haruto. Even as a grown man, Haruto still did as Mother told him. There were plenty of times when outsiders thought them odd for it, but still, they raised Yuta to call Naomi 'Mama'.

. . .

Raising a child again after so long was difficult, but she found so much fun and joy in it, too. Seeing Yuta grow up thrilled her, and Haruto shared her happiness. She never dreamed those days would end.

But always, when she was cuddling Yuta, or feeding him, or playing with him at the park, a dark shadow of guilt loomed over her.

It was a first for her.

Long ago, when she had broken her mother's neck, Naomi had not felt even a hint of remorse. Because she had been defending Cheepy. For Naomi, justice had been on her side.

The same had been true for her husband, and Iwata, and Toyokawa. She knew what she had done was wrong, but she had no regrets. It had all been to protect Haruto.

Every time she had sinned, it had been to protect someone. Like a mother bear protecting her cubs, Naomi had killed those men out of love and justice.

But . . . What about this time?

How had she felt, giving Yuki those salt pills?

Naomi knew the truth. This time, she had committed murder for her own selfish reasons.

I want to be a mother forever. I never want to lose the right to that name, Mother. That alone was her reason for murdering that kind young woman, the woman Haruto had loved.

She knew she would pay for it, somehow.

.　　.　　.

When the payment fell due, it was unannounced.

One morning she awoke and found that Haruto was gone from his futon beside hers. Anxiety filled her breast.

Naomi leapt up and searched their apartment. She found him hanging by the neck, dead.

She didn't find a note in his room, but later, she found something like one. On the internet.

Haruto had left a post on the blog he'd kept before his death, a few days before his suicide.

I am going to stop updating this blog today.
I've finally figured out the secret of those three drawings.
I can't imagine the kind of pain you must have been suffering.
Nor can I understand the depths of whatever sin you committed.
I cannot forgive you. But even so, I will always love you.

Raku

He had written it for Naomi.

She discovered what he meant by 'those three drawings' after looking back through the blog.

An old woman pulling a baby out of his dead mother's womb. The old woman was clearly Naomi.

Yuki had understood. She had seen the murder lurking in Naomi's heart.

But when? Naomi recalled a day, about a week before the due date, when Yuki had suddenly broken down crying. She had wept for hours, like the world was ending. That might have been it.

If Naomi's plan had been more direct, perhaps she could have asked Haruto for help. She could have gone to the police.

But Naomi's methods were so very subtle. There is no crime in filling capsules with salt and giving them to someone. If anyone had found out, it would have been simple to talk her way out of it.

And Haruto, who trusted Naomi more than anyone, who clung to her even as an adult, would have believed anything Naomi said. Yuki would simply have become the villain, a horrible wife who had accused her mother-in-law of plotting a murder. She could never have stayed in this home.

She was estranged from her parents, unemployed and no longer young. She had nowhere to go.

And so, Yuki had pretended she didn't know that Naomi wanted her dead.

Even with high blood pressure, the chances of a woman dying in childbirth were relatively low. Yuki had probably thought she would be fine. Surely she didn't believe she would actually die.

But, on the off-chance that Naomi's plan did indeed work, she had left behind those pictures, containing a coded message, without knowing when Haruto would even notice it, if he ever did.

It had taken Haruto three years from Yuki's death to break her code.

That day, Haruto understood the meaning of those pictures.

The anguish he had felt then was painfully clear in his note.

'I cannot forgive you.' Of course he couldn't. She had taken his beloved wife from him.

'But even so, I will always love you.' He did not hate his mother. That was how powerful a presence Naomi was in Haruto's heart.

The conflict between those feelings drove Haruto to take his own life.

Naomi finally saw the mistake she had made in raising her son.

She had surely loved Haruto more than anyone, done more for him than anyone, but in doing so she had stood in the way of his independence. It was as if Haruto's umbilical cord had never been cut. No matter how old he grew, he remained always a part of Naomi. So, no matter how hatefully she might have acted, he could not resent her. He could not break free of her.

'Haruto . . . I'm so sorry.'

Naomi sat in front of the family Buddhist altar and whispered her apology over and over again. But the tears would not come.

When faced with true sorrow, people lose even the strength to shed tears.

Isamu Kumai

Touching his belly through the bandage, Kumai barely felt any pain at all. He was shocked at his own recovery.

But no matter how quickly his wound healed, his body was still being consumed, moment by moment.

He'd found out three weeks before.

'Mr Kumai, this is difficult to say, but . . . it's come back. Stage two oesophageal cancer. It's still operable, but the five-year survival rate is only fifty per cent,' his doctor had told him at his last regular health check.

On the way home that day, Kumai had looked back over his life.

He'd worked hard as a young reporter. He'd been proud of his work back then. He'd believed it was valuable to society. But now, he doubted everything about his own past.

Did I ever help anyone? No matter how many articles I might write, it's the police who arrest the bad guy. Reporters just tag along after the cops, trying to sell whatever scraps of information they let slip. Twenty years ago, all I did was work myself half to death to satisfy the curiosity of a bunch of snoops.

And then he remembered a certain young man.

Now Iwata, on the other hand . . . He got it right, more than I ever did. He found the truth before even the cops did. He found the murderer, and even as he was about to die, made sure to leave a clue. My twenty years, and his few weeks. Which of these was more valuable?

It rankled him.

He couldn't stand the thought of dying with Iwata out ahead.

If he wanted to beat Iwata, there was only one way to do it.

He had to catch Naomi.

·   ·   ·

That day, Kumai headed out for the L— Prefecture Police Headquarters for a meeting.

The man he went to meet was named Keizo Kurata. Back when Kumai was a reporter, he'd been Kumai's most cooperative detective. They were around the same age and grew up in the same region, so they'd sometimes broken down the detective–reporter barrier and actually enjoyed a drink together. Kurata seemed happy to be getting together again after so long.

'Hey, Kumai! Good to see you again. How've you been?'

'Can't complain. You're looking fit, Kurata.'

'I am that! Listen, we just had a grandchild! Hope I make it to see his wedding! Hahaha!'

'Congratulations to you! Let's both not kick the bucket yet, then.'

'Thank you, thank you. So, what brings you all the way out here?'

'Right. So, I wanted to get your opinion on something. What are the chances of getting a homicide investigation reopened on a case from 1992 and 1995?'

'What months?'

'Both incidents in September.'

'Well, 1992 is already past the statute of limitations. But September 1995 is still valid, thanks to some legal reforms. But a case that old, the investigating team's already been broken up. You couldn't get it reopened without some new evidence.'

'You don't have the authority to get things moving?'

'Come on, a sergeant doesn't have that kind of pull!'

'I've got a lead. With modern techniques, I think we could turn up some evidence.'

'Sorry, but "could" won't get things moving.'

'Right. What if we got the suspect arrested?'

'What are you talking about?'

'Let's just say, for the sake of speculation, that the murderer in those cases happened to stab me with a kitchen knife. And you just happened to be in the vicinity and caught them red-handed. In that case, you'd start looking into possible crimes they'd committed in the past, right?'

'So, if they were arrested on a separate charge, you mean? Of course, we'd have to start looking into other possible offences. But for that to happen, first of all, you'd have to get yourself stabbed by this culprit, right?'

'I would. So I'm going to have to goad her into it.'

'Goad her . . . ? You mean, you know who it is?'

'I do. I don't have the proof yet, but I'm not wrong. So listen, Kurata, I'm asking you as a favour. Come to the scene and arrest her for me.'

'Hey, just hold on a minute. Let's think this through calmly.'

'I am calm. I'm saying this with a clear head. I want that murderer caught. I have to do it. It's like it's my final duty.'

'But do you have to do it in such a reckless way? This way, the slightest mistake and you're a dead man, right?'

'I'm not worried about that. To tell the truth . . . the cancer's back.'

'What?'

'If I get an operation, there's only a fifty-fifty chance I'll live through the next five years. And even if I do survive, all I've got waiting for me is a lonely death. I've got no wife, no kids. No grandkids, of course. So, please. Help me. Think of it as saving me, if you want. Let me die having done something of value for once.'

226

Kurata paused. Then said, 'Can you wait a bit for an answer?'

A few days later, Kurata rang him up.

He would do as Kumai had asked. But on one condition.

'You have to wear a vest. You can't die. Promise me!'

.   .   .

On April 20, 2015, Kumai took a room at a Tokyo hotel.

At around five in the evening, he put on a grey coat and went out. He hid in the shadows outside a convenience store in a quiet residential neighbourhood.

He waited for around thirty minutes, then a parent and child passed by. He checked their faces and was sure. It was Naomi Konno. Kumai went after them. A few minutes after he started trailing them, Naomi glanced back.

That was quick . . .

It drove home just how sharp a person's senses could become after living in fear of the police for twenty years.

Kumai's plan was a simple one. He wanted to scare Naomi.

He wanted her to think someone was after them. If she felt the child was in danger, he knew Naomi would bare her teeth. She would try to kill again.

On the 22nd, Kumai parked his black hire car at the convenience store and waited for Naomi and Yuta. Suddenly his heart started racing.

As the Konnos walked past the front of his car, he got a clear look at Naomi's profile in the light of the setting sun. Her face was layered in make-up, creating a facade of youth. But her expression was filled with kindness. It was the face of a mother watching over her young child.

Kumai fought his own hesitancy and stepped on the accelerator.

Those people you killed had families, too.

On the fourth day of his tail, Naomi's fear was clearly deeper than before. She pulled at the child's hand and ran into the lobby of her building. Kumai followed them to their apartment on the sixth floor, trying to stoke her fear even more. When he saw her hands trembling as she unlocked the door, and the way she burst inside, he knew his chance had come.

He called Kurata on the spot.

'We'll do it tomorrow evening.'

.   .   .

The following evening, Kumai spent longer than usual soaking in the hotel bath, then slowly drank a cup of coffee. Then he donned his grey coat.

He didn't put on the protective vest. The worse his injury, the heavier Naomi's sentence. It would be even harsher if he ended up dying.

Grey's a good colour for a burial shroud. Very fitting.

He laughed at himself.

That night, he met Kurata in front of the apartment building, and the two of them went up to the sixth floor.

Kurata waited around the corner in the hallway as Kumai rang the Konno family's doorbell.

Soon a voice called out from the other side.

'Yes, I'm coming!' It was filled with false levity.

On April 24th, Naomi Konno was arrested for assault with a deadly weapon. Police are pursuing investigations into her possible connection with multiple past murders. Konno says—

Tomiko Hagio put the newspaper down on the table and tried to calm herself with a sip of bottled tea. Her armpits were clammy with sweat.

'Naomi? But . . . Why?'

Hagio opened a cabinet in her office. It held box after box containing the case files from her time as a counsellor. After hours of searching, she found the drawing she was looking for.

It had been drawn by a little girl named Naomi Konno, who had been taken into custody for killing her mother many, many years ago.

Hagio had once looked at this picture and judged that the girl was fit for rehabilitation.

The sharp thorns on the branches represented Naomi's defiant and aggressive nature. But there was an adorable little bird drawn in a tree's hollow.

It expresses her kindness in wanting to protect weak creatures. Giving her contact with animals could nurture her maternal instincts and gradually soften that defiance and aggression.

That was the diagnosis Hagio had made.

But . . . as she looked at it now, the possibility of a different interpretation arose.

Taking care of something weaker—like a child—might well have worsened her innate aggression.

Could those thorns be there to protect the bird?

A personality that could cause any amount of injury to an enemy if it meant protecting a weaker creature . . . Could that tree actually represent Naomi Konno, serial killer, herself?

Hagio's whole body began shivering. She was ashamed of her past short-sightedness.

If she asked Naomi to draw a similar picture today, what would it look like? What manner of thorns would be sprouting from the tree in her heart now?

Isamu Kumai

'All right. It's all closed up now. No need for these bandages, dear! I think you'll be discharged tomorrow.' The nurse turned and danced out through the door, her nasal voice ringing through the room.

So, goodbye, boring white ceiling.

The thought held a touch of sadness.

Then a voice came from beyond the bedside curtain.

'Mr Kumai, it sounds like you'll be leaving soon. Congrats.'

The voice belonged to the young man who'd come in with a broken leg a few days ago. Kumai wasn't fond of talking about himself, but the boy's peculiar tone had somehow loosened his tongue. The last few days, he'd shared all kinds of things. About his time working at the newspaper, the stories he'd done as a reporter and his own stage two cancer.

'Thanks.'

'But it does sound rough. As soon as you get out, you'll have to come right back in for cancer surgery.'

'No, no surgery for me.'

'Why not? It's not terminal, is it?'

'I'm already sixty-five. Even if I managed to hang on for a bit longer, there's not much of a life waiting for me. Didn't I tell you? I don't have any family. Not a lot of fun in living out my days alone.'

'There's fun to be had, even living alone. You could try scuba diving or bouldering or something.'

'Oh, come on, don't get smart with me.'

'And I think you've still got something left to do.'

'What might that be?'

'You were part of Naomi Konno's arrest. Now, you need to look after her grandson, Yuta.'

His heart skipped a beat. He hadn't said a word about that case to the boy.

'H-hey, wait a second. How do you know about that?'

'I saw it on the news. "Newspaper employee Isamu Kumai risks his life to catch the suspect in multiple unsolved murders."'

It was quite a shock when I saw your name on the hospital room door when I checked in. Imagine, someone like that in the bed next to me!'

'You should have said something, if you knew all along . . .'

So he had, in the end, made the national news. Maybe it wasn't so odd for the young man in the next bed to have known about it.

'But it was a good thing. Catching Naomi Konno. Now Mr Iwata and Mr Toyokawa can rest in peace.'

'What was that?'

That wasn't right.

The police hadn't released those details. There was no way a normal citizen could know about Iwata and Toyokawa.

'Are you working with the police or something? Or are you a reporter?'

'No.'

'Then how do you know those names?'

'I just did some digging on my own. You can find anything on the internet these days. Naomi Konno's husband Yoshiharu Miura, murdered in 1992. Then, three years later, the murderer killed Shunsuke Iwata in the same way. And now one of the key figures in those cases, Naomi Konno, has been arrested. It's not hard to connect the dots.'

'Well, if you put it like that.'

'I also saw the pictures that Iwata and Miura drew before they died. They clearly couldn't see what they were doing when they were drawing. I wondered what was going on there, but it's pretty simple to guess since the sleeping bags were gone. They were attacked while they were asleep.'

'Who on earth are you?'

'I'm just a student.'

'How does "just a student" know so much about some old murders?'

'The truth is, last year I was tipped off to a very odd blog. I couldn't stop thinking about it, and for the past year I've been spending all my time digging into it. And then, all of a sudden, I found that it was linked to this case. Did you know about that, Mr Kumai? Naomi Konno's son's blog?'

'No . . . I had no idea.'

'Well then, I might be able to give you a scoop. If you read it carefully, I think you'll discover another of Naomi Konno's crimes. I believe she's responsible for the death of her daughter-in-law.'

Kumai was dumbstruck.

Naomi's daughter-in-law, Yuki Konno, had died in 2009. He didn't think the boy was making things up.

'Listen, Mr Kumai. Let's make a deal.'

'What kind of deal?'

'I'll tell you the name of the blog, and in return you do something for me.'

'And what might that be?'

'Get the surgery.'

'What good will my getting the surgery do you?'

'Not me, for Yuta Konno. Like I said. I think you should look after Yuta until he grows up. Catching the murderer doesn't mean it's all over. Nothing will be over until Yuta, who's lost everyone close to him, can live a happy life.'

It was true. Kumai had been thinking about Yuta, too. With Naomi in prison, the boy was living in an orphanage. He must be so lonely. And if Kumai hadn't chased Naomi down, it wouldn't have gone that way. He didn't regret what he'd done, but he did feel some sense of responsibility.

'I have been thinking I owe the boy something myself.'

'Then it sounds like a win-win to me. Do we have a deal?'

'Fine. You win. I'll get the surgery.'

'Great!'

'So, tell me. What's the title?'

'It's called *Oh No, not Raku!*'

'Wait a minute. Don't go playing tricks on me. Naomi Konno's son was named Haruto Konno. Not Raku!'

'It's a pen name. Kind of a tricky one, in fact. First, spell out Haruto Konno in Roman letters and then mix them up to make new words. It's an anagram . . .'

HARUTO KONNO

OHNONOTRAKU

'Some kind of word game? And you figured that out? Not bad.'

'Thank you. So, I've kept my side of the bargain. Now, it's your turn. Make sure to get that surgery once you check out of here, please.'

'Fine, fine. I'm a man of my word. But tell me one more thing. Why are you so hung up on this case? Did you really go that far just 'cause you're curious? Sorry to put it this way, but are you some kind of snoop?'

'A while ago, an older student at my college, a club member, told me that when I figured out the story of that blog, I should tell him about it. He's already graduated, but I want to be able to keep that promise next time we meet. And to be able to do that, the case has to be all cleared up. Otherwise, where's the fun in talking about it?'

·   ·   ·

One sunny day at the end of June 2015.

Miu Yonezawa's father has been bustling his brawny frame around the garden of their house from dawn, sweat pouring as he gets the charcoal burning. He spreads out a feast of fish, vegetables and beef on the sizzling grill. Miu takes up her favourite bits and savours each bite, dunking them in sauce.

'Miu, don't just fill up on meat. Eat your veggies, too!'

'I know, I know,' she says, as she puts a fresh piece of meat in her mouth.

Nearby, his wife sits in a garden chair and watches them.

The truth is, the Yonezawas were planning on hosting the Konno family today. But then, well, all that bad business happened. Since Naomi was arrested, Yuta has been living in an orphanage. He must be so lonely, so anxious, they thought. They wanted to do something for him, to make him feel better, so they invited him to the barbecue.

And suddenly, Miu cries out, 'Oh! It's Yuta!'

They look towards the gate, and there Yuta stands. He arrives with an older man. His name is Kumai, and he's volunteering to look after Yuta. They don't know how he's related to the boy, but they have heard that he's started the adoption process.

Mr Yonezawa hurries over to the pair. 'Hey! Yuta! Welcome, welcome!'

Yuta gives a little bow in greeting.

'And thank you for coming with him, Mr Kumai. Why don't you have some food?'

'I appreciate the offer, but I'm afraid I can't. I recently had surgery and can't really stomach much these days.'

'Oh dear, I'm sorry to hear that.'

'I'll be nearby killing time. Give me a ring when you're finished.

There's no rush, though. Enjoy!' Kumai says, and walks away, one hand in his pocket.

.   .   .

Yuta stands with a plate in his hand, not taking any food. He is probably too nervous. 'Yuta, what kind of meat do you like?' Mr Yonezawa asks, his voice full of pep. 'We've got thick juicy steaks. Thin, tender slices, and meat on the bone, too. I'll cook whatever you'd like, so just say the word!'

Yuta stands and fidgets, his lips pressed. Miu butts in.

'Listen, Papa, Yuta doesn't really like meat much.'

'What?! Well, how rude of me! Sorry about that, Yuta. I guess there's not much here for you to eat.'

'But he does love stir-fried noodles. Don't you, Yuta?'

Yuta nods shyly.

'Right! Then I shall get to stir frying!'

He removes the grill and lays a metal plate over the coals. He tears up some cabbage and begins cooking it with a packet of noodles.

Miu and Yuta stand watching him expectantly.

Yonezawa knows. Children are more sensitive to sadness and anxiety than adults. And, much like adults, they try desperately to hide it from those around them. Miu and Yuta must both surely be suffering behind those smiles. And that is why Yonezawa is so intent on showing the two of them that, for all life's pain, there is just as much fun and joy to be found. He fills his voice with cheer.

'All right. Yuta! Miu! Just you wait. I am going to make you the most delicious noodles the world has ever seen!'

236

ABOUT THE AUTHOR

Uketsu only ever appears online, wearing a mask and speaking through a voice changer.

He has more than 1.5 million followers.

His innovative 'sketch mysteries' challenge readers to discover the hidden clues in a series of sinister drawings.

They have sold nearly 3 million copies in Japan since 2021.

Translation rights have been sold in twenty-seven languages and counting.

Uketsu's true name and identity remain unknown.

Here ends Uketsu's
Strange Pictures.

The first edition of this book was printed
and bound at Lakeside Book Company
in Harrisonburg, Virginia, in December 2024.

A NOTE ON THE TYPE

The text of this novel was set in Dante MT Pro, Ron
Carpenter's digital rendering of the popular typeface
designed by Giovanni Marderstei. Influenced by the
Monotype Bembo and Centaur typefaces, Mardersteig
wanted to design a font that balanced italic and roman
harmoniously. Originally hand-cut by Charles Malin, it
was adapted for mechanical composition by Monotype
in 1957. Dante remains a popular typeface today, and it
appears especially elegant on the printed page.

HarperVia

An imprint dedicated to publishing international voices,
offering readers a chance to encounter other lives and other
points of view via the language of the imagination.